The Vanishing Thieves

With his heart pounding, Joe watched the fin going around again, this time in a narrower circle. The shark had spotted him when it originally went by, and was now closing in.

He submerged in order to get an underwater look at the beast. An enormous man-eating white shark over twenty feet long passed him no more than a dozen feet away.

Surfacing, Joe watched as the great fin cut the water in a wide arc that took it fifty yards beyond him, then swung back in his direction. This time it moved in a straight line, directly toward him!

The Hardy Boys Mystery Stories

Available from MINSTREL Books

66

The HARDY BOYS®

THE VANISHING THIEVES

FRANKLIN W. DIXON

A MINSTREL® BOOK

PUBLISHED BY POCKET BOOKS

New York   London   Toronto   Sydney   Tokyo   Singapore

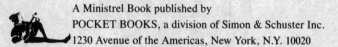 A Ministrel Book published by
POCKET BOOKS, a division of Simon & Schuster Inc.
1230 Avenue of the Americas, New York, N.Y. 10020

Copyright © 1981 by Simon & Schuster Inc.
Front cover illustration by Daniel Horne

ISBN: 0-671-63890-4

First Ministrel Books printing February 1989

10 9 8 7 6 5 4 3

Printed in the U.S.A.

Contents

1 The Stolen Car

"Quick, eat the rest of the pizza!" Frank Hardy urged. "Here comes Chet!"

It was Saturday afternoon and Frank and his younger brother Joe were seated at a table in the Bayport Diner with Callie Shaw and Iola Morton. Iola's tubby brother Chet, who was known for his voracious appetite, and a slender boy of about eighteen had just walked in.

Frank's warning was too late. Chet had already spotted them, and was headed their way with his gaze fixed on the half-eaten pizza. His companion followed close behind.

Picking up a piece of pie, Chet said, "Umm, pepperoni and cheese, my favorite."

"You're welcome," Joe said with good-humored sarcasm.

After taking a bite, Chet turned to the other boy, and in a generous tone offered, "Have some pizza, Vern."

"No, thanks," Vern said, embarrassed.

"Chet, you might at least introduce Vern before eating up everything in sight," Iola admonished her brother.

"Oh, sure," Chet said. "This is our cousin, Vern Nelson, from Canada." He used his slice of pizza as a pointer. "Callie Shaw, Frank and Joe Hardy."

"Vern is visiting us at the farm," Iola explained.

Finishing his piece of pizza, Chet took another. "The matinee today is a monster movie," he announced. "Why don't we all go?"

The others agreed, and a few minutes later the six left the diner. As they emerged onto the parking lot, Vern Nelson suddenly stopped short. "Somebody's stealing my car!" he cried out.

A brand-new blue sedan was being driven out of the lot by a red-haired man. "Let's go after him!" Chet cried.

The young people raced to the Hardys' sports sedan and jumped in. Frank, Callie, and Vern sat in front, while the others squeezed into the back. Seconds later, Frank began following the blue sedan.

The thief had a head start of a block, but was

2

not driving fast. Frank soon reduced the distance between them to a quarter of a block. However, intervening traffic kept him from getting any closer.

The red-haired man obviously was unaware that he was being followed, because he kept well within the speed limit. He headed for the downtown section of Bayport. Frank gradually narrowed the distance between them until he was only fifty feet behind. At that moment, the thief seemed to realize he was being tailed. Suddenly he floored the accelerator!

There was a red light ahead. The man drove through it with a blasting horn, barely missing another car. Frank had to brake to a halt, and though the light changed a moment later, the stolen car was already more than a block away.

Frank saw the thief turn left into an alley. He went after him, but when he emerged at the next cross street, there was no sign of the blue sedan.

A huge eighteen-wheel truck was parked on the right, and the driver was closing the back door. Joe called out to him, "Did you see a blue sedan speed by here?"

The driver turned around. He was a squat, powerfully built man wearing a short-sleeved sport shirt that revealed tattooed arms.

"Zoomed by like an express train," he said. He pointed east. "Went that way."

"Thanks," Joe said, as Frank turned the car in that direction.

The thief, however, was nowhere to be found. They cruised up and down side streets for a time, then drove to the Hardy home on Elm Street. All thoughts of a movie matinee were now abandoned.

Aunt Gertrude was in the kitchen when the six young people trooped in the back door. Miss Hardy, sister of the boys' father, was a tall, angular, peppery woman, who was just taking a pie from the oven.

"Umm, smells like cherry," Chet said, moving towards the pastry.

"This is no time to think about food," Joe told him. "We have to call the police."

"The police!" Aunt Gertrude repeated. "Are you boys involved with criminals again?"

"Tell you all about it later," Frank promised, heading into the front hall.

He used the front hall extension to call Chief of Police Ezra Collig. Fenton Hardy came down the stairs as he was talking. The tall, middle-aged detective had once been with the New York City police force, but was now a world-famous private investigator.

"What's going on?" he asked Frank as his oldest son hung up.

4

Frank introduced Vern Nelson to his father and then explained about the car theft.

"That's quite a coincidence," Mr. Hardy said. "I happen to be investigating a car-theft ring, but not in this area."

"Where are they operating?" Joe asked.

"Mainly in New York City."

Chet said, "The funny thing is the way the car disappeared. Course that red light slowed us down, but we were only a little over a block behind when the thief turned into the alley. He should have still been in sight when we came out the other end."

"Particularly since that tattooed fellow told us which way he went," Vern Nelson said.

"Tattooed fellow?" Fenton Hardy asked, raising his eyebrows.

"A truck driver," Frank explained. "He was closing up the back of his truck when we drove up."

"What did he look like?"

"Sort of squat, but well-built."

"Did you happen to notice the design of his tattoos?"

The four boys and Iola had not paid any attention, but Callie Shaw said, "I saw the one on his right arm as we went by. It was a dagger with a snake wrapped around it."

"Crafty Kraft!" the detective exclaimed. "The

car-theft ring must be spreading, because he's one of its chief lieutenants!"

"You mean that driver's in cahoots with the gang you're investigating?" Joe asked in surprise.

Mr. Hardy nodded. "I've a feeling Vern's car disappeared into Kraft's truck. It's probably the type whose rear door lowers to form a driving ramp."

"Oh!" Vern said in exasperation. "I wish I could lay my hands on him and that redheaded thief who drove off in my new car!"

"The car thief was red-haired?" Fenton Hardy asked.

"Yes."

"Now I'm positive it was the gang I'm after," the detective said. "Red Sluice, one of the slickest car-heist artists in the country, works with Crafty Kraft."

Mr. Hardy listened to the group's description of the truck, and phoned the information to Chief Collig. When he hung up, Vern asked whether he thought there was a chance his car would be found.

"I doubt it," the detective said frankly. "So far not a single vehicle suspected of being stolen by this ring has been recovered. The theory is that they're either being repainted and sold in other states under fake registrations, or being stripped for spare parts."

"But the police have the truck's description."

The detective nodded. "But no license number, and there are hundreds of similar trucks on the highways."

Aunt Gertrude walked in from the kitchen and invited the boys' friends for dinner. They all accepted, and, after calling their parents, went into the dining room.

With Mrs. Hardy, there were nine around the table. Laura Hardy was a slim, attractive woman with sparkling blue eyes. She quickly put Vern at ease by warmly asking about his family and plans for his stay in Bayport.

Vern explained that he was an orphan who lived with an older sister in Montreal. An uncle on his father's side—no relation to the Mortons—had died in California and had left him a rare coin, a 1913 Liberty Head nickel. Only five of those were known to be in existence, and his Uncle Gregg, who had bought his eight years ago, had paid $100,000 for it. However, the coin had disappeared under mysterious circumstances before the will could be probated. Vern was on his way to California to look into the matter, and had stopped en route to visit the Mortons.

"Was the coin stolen?" Fenton Hardy asked.

"That's the mystery," Vern replied. "According to the will, it was supposed to be in a safe-deposit box in Los Angeles. But when the box was opened, it was not there. Only Uncle Gregg had a key, and the vault record showed that he had not visited it since the day he placed the coin in it eight years ago."

"That sounds like a case for the Hardy boys," Chet said. "Why don't the three of us go to California with you?"

"I no longer have a car to get there," Vern remarked.

"Maybe we could fly," Frank suggested.

"You're going to get involved with criminals again?" Aunt Gertrude asked in a worried tone. "Must you?"

"Don't worry about it, Aunt Gertrude," Joe said cheerfully. "We can take care of ourselves."

"So far. But someday you may get in more trouble than you can handle."

"We'll be careful," Frank assured her.

Laura Hardy asked, "Why are there only five of these coins in existence, Vern? Nineteen-thirteen isn't that long ago. I think I have a 1910 nickel in a drawer somewhere myself."

"They were not a regular issue and were never placed in circulation," the boy replied. "The story is that a group of VIPs was visiting the mint, and to show them how it operated, 1913 Liberty Head nickels were cast. As the government switched from the Liberty Head to the Indian Head nickel that year, no other Liberty Heads were ever minted. The coins were supposed to be destroyed after the demonstration, but half of them disappeared while the visitors were examining them."

"You mean they were stolen!" Mrs. Hardy exclaimed. "Who were these visitors?"

"All reputable men," Vern said with a grin. "They included a senator, a cabinet officer, and a general. Years later, five coins showed up in the estate of a well-known millionaire. Those five were sold by the estate, and eventually my uncle bought one."

A loud thud sounded, seeming to come from the front hall. Frank went to investigate. When he saw nothing amiss, he opened the front door.

The point of a large dagger was buried in the heavy oak, pinning a note to the wood. Penned in block letters was: IF YOU WANT YOUR FAMILY TO STAY HEALTHY, DROP YOUR INVESTIGATION, HARDY.

9

2 Hijacked!

When Frank shouted in surprise, everyone at the dinner table rushed into the front hall to see what was going on.

"I'll bet that was left by the car-theft gang," Joe remarked, after reading the note.

"Not necessarily," Mr. Hardy said. "That isn't the only case I'm working on. Let's see if the culprit left his fingerprints."

Using a handkerchief, the detective pulled the dagger from the door and carried it to his laboratory. The four boys followed, while the girls stayed to help Mrs. Hardy and Aunt Gertrude clear the table.

Holding the dagger with forceps, Mr. Hardy used

a camel's hair brush to dust it lightly with a fine, dark powder. A set of prints appeared on the haft. He lifted them off with inch-wide transparent tape and transferred them onto a white card.

Then he took a number of case folders from a filing cabinet and compared fingerprint cards in them to the prints taken from the dagger. After checking the first folder, he shook his head.

"It isn't any known member of the car-theft gang," he said.

He examined several other folders without success. Finally he exclaimed triumphantly, "Anton Jivaro! I didn't even know he was still in the States. He was supposed to have fled to Canada."

"Who's Anton Jivaro?" Frank asked.

"An escaped mental patient. A clever man, but insane. Thinks he is the Maharaja of Kashmir, and has a nasty habit of hijacking planes to take him to India. I caught him once, that's why I have his prints on file."

"Maybe you'd better turn on the outside lights and the burglar alarm tonight," Joe suggested. "Just in case Jivaro decides to come back with another dagger."

"Good idea," Mr. Hardy said.

When they returned to the kitchen, Aunt Gertrude was horrified to learn that the dagger had been left by a madman.

11

"We'll all be murdered in our sleep," she declared. "Why do you take such cases, Fenton?"

"I'll turn the alarm and the outside lights on," her brother assured her. "Don't worry, nothing will happen."

While Mr. Hardy and the boys had been busy in the laboratory, Laura Hardy had hunted up the 1910 Liberty Head nickel she owned. She showed it to Vern.

After examining it, he said, "It isn't worth very much, Mrs. Hardy. Maybe fifty cents or a dollar. I could tell you exactly if I had my bible with me."

"Your bible?"

"The annual Guide Book of United States Coins. Coin collectors call it the bible."

"It's at our house," Chet said. "If we fly to Los Angeles, put it in your hand luggage. That way we can check our pocket change on the plane."

After some discussion, it was decided that Frank, Joe, Chet, and Vern would go to Los Angeles the next day. Everyone was very exhausted from the excitement of the day, and Frank and Joe drove all of their guests home. Filled with anticipation, both boys had trouble sleeping.

The following morning, as they waited in line at Bayport Airport, Chet called attention to a dark, furtive-looking little man who had bought a ticket.

"Hope they check that fellow for guns," he said

forebodingly. "He looks like a hijacker to me."

"You watch too many movies," Frank scoffed.

Walking over to the security checkpoint, they found themselves standing right behind the dark little man. When he passed through without causing the electronic metal detector to buzz, Chet was relieved. "I guess he doesn't have a gun on him after all," he said.

Then Chet passed through. A bulb lit up and there was a loud buzz. Immediately two security officers grabbed him. While one gripped him firmly from behind, the other patted his pants pockets, then reached into the left one. He drew out a metal box.

"Open it!" he commanded.

Sheepishly Chet obeyed. Inside was a large collection of nickels.

"Why are you carrying your change in a metal box?" the guard demanded.

"It's kind of my piggy bank," Chet replied with wounded dignity.

The guard shook his head, handed back the box, and passed the boy through. As the four friends moved toward the gate, Vern inquired why his cousin was loaded down with nickels.

"I didn't have time to check them last night, so I thought I'd do it on the plane. Did you bring your bible?"

"Sure. But what do you expect to find?"

"Maybe a 1913 Liberty Head nickel!"

On the plane Frank, Joe, and Vern sat in one row, while Chet's seat was across the aisle, next to an attractive, platinum blond woman of about thirty. Beside her, in the window seat, was the dark little man Chet had suspected of being a hijacker.

When they were airborne, Chet took out a handful of nickels and began checking their dates. After a while the platinum blonde asked curiously, "Do you mind telling me what you're doing?"

"Looking for a particular coin, ma'am."

"Oh."

Frank, who was on the aisle seat across from Chet, leaned forward with a grin and said, "He's a little odd, ma'am, but harmless. Don't mind him."

She smiled. "You four all together?"

"Yes, we are."

"Well then, let's get acquainted. It's a long flight. I'm Cylvia Nash."

"How do you do?" Frank said. "I'm Frank Hardy, and our friend next to you is Chet Morton. On my left are my brother Joe, and Vern Nelson."

"Glad to meet you," Cylvia Nash said. "You boys on vacation?"

"Not exactly," Chet said, dropping the nickels into an empty pocket and taking another handful out of his "piggy bank." "Didn't you recognize the names Frank and Joe Hardy?"

The woman shook her head, puzzled, while the man next to her openly stared at them.

"Fenton Hardy's sons," Chet explained.

"Oh, the famous private detective." She looked at Frank and Joe admiringly. "You often help your father, don't you? Are you on a case now?"

"We are," Chet replied. "You see, this valuable coin disappeared—"

"It's really not a case at all," Frank interrupted, giving Chet a sharp glance. "A relative lost something and we're going to try and find it. Since we haven't been to California in a long time, we're really looking forward to it."

"Yes, we want to get some sightseeing in," Joe added.

"You'll like it," Cylvia said. "Are you planning to visit the northern part of the state, too?"

"We don't know yet," Frank said. "Do you live near there?"

"No, L.A. I'm returning from vacation."

The dark little man on her right said, "Excuse me, madam, but do you know how to work this?" He held up his earphone for recorded music.

As Cylvia Nash showed him how to plug it in, Chet resumed examining nickels.

"Hey!" he exlaimed. "I found a 1901 Liberty

Head!" Leaning across the aisle, he said to his cousin, "That worth anything, Vern?"

"Let's see it," Vern requested.

Chet passed the coin across the aisle to Frank, who handed it to Vern. After studying the nickel, Vern took a small red book from his pocket and opened it.

"Twenty-six-and-a-half million of those coins were minted," he stated. "If it were a proof coin, it would be worth a hundred and thirty-five dollars. If you could find a buyer, that is, which is unlikely unless you're a dealer. A dealer would probably give you about half that."

"I'll settle for sixty-five dollars," Chet said eagerly. "Is it a proof coin?"

Vern shook his head. "The next grade down is uncirculated. That's worth seventy-two-fifty, again about half that from a dealer."

"Is it uncirculated?"

"No. Now extra-fine grade would bring about six dollars from a dealer."

"What grade is it?" Chet asked meekly.

Studying it again, Vern said, "It has some worn spots, so it can't be rated very fine, or even fine. Very good is the next rating down, but I don't think it's even that. I'd say it rates only as good."

"So what's that worth?"

"You might get thirty cents for it."

Chet made a face. "Big deal!" He took the nickel and dropped all of the coins into his metal box.

Cylvia Nash, who had been listening, leaned forward to Vern. "You seem to know a lot about coins, young man."

"My uncle was a collector, and he taught me. Are you interested in numismatics?"

She shook her head. "I know nothing about the subject."

Just then the little man next to her unplugged his earphone. "Thanks again for showing me how to use this," he said.

"You're welcome," she replied. "We haven't introduced ourselves. I'm Cylvia Nash."

"How do you do?" he said formally. "I am the Maharaja of Kashmir."

Chet stiffened. Trying not to show his excitement, he signaled Frank to meet him at the back of the plane.

Both boys pretended to go toward the restroom. As soon as they were beyond earshot of the others, Chet whispered, "That little guy is Anton Jivaro, the hijacker! I heard him tell Miss Nash he was the Maharaja of Kashmir!"

Frank stared at him. "Are you sure?"

"Of course I am."

"Then we better get word to the captain that there is a mental patient aboard," Frank decided.

"Well, at least he doesn't have a gun," Chet said. "He couldn't have sneaked it past that detector."

Jivaro had risen from his seat and stepped past Cylvia Nash into the aisle. In a loud voice, he said, "May I have everyone's attention?"

Most conversation stopped and all the passengers looked at him questioningly. He opened his coat, then slowly made a complete turn so that everyone could see the six long, brownish-colored tubes strapped to his waist.

"These are sticks of dynamite," he announced. He took hold of the loop at the end of a short lanyard attached to his belt and wrapped it around his hand. "If I pull this, the explosives will go off."

There was dead silence in the plane.

"If everyone behaves, I will not have to use them," he continued. "I don't wish to harm you. I only want to be flown to my native land. You see, I am the Maharaja of Kashmir."

Silence continued. The hijacker's gaze fixed on the flight attendant who had just emerged from the small galley at the rear of the plane.

"Stewardess!" he demanded. "Take me to your captain!" Turning to the passengers, he gently raised his hand with the lanyard wrapped around it. "Remember, don't anybody try anything. I can pull this in a second . . . and I'll blow us all up if I have to!"

3 Crash Landing

As the hijacker and the flight attendant disappeared into the cockpit, Cylvia Nash said in a high voice, "Kashmir? Where in the world is that?"

"On the northern border of India," Frank replied, looking around at the stunned passengers.

Joe tried to break the tension. "My brother's been reading up on the Far East," he spoke up.

"Yes? Well, who is the real Maharaja of Kashmir?" Chet asked.

"There isn't any. Kashmir used to be an independent nation ruled by an absolute monarch, but after World War II, both India and Pakistan tried to take it over. In 1956, India formally annexed it, but Pakistan still claims it. An assembly set up by the United Nations in 1949 abolished the monarchy. I don't know if the man who was maharaja at that time is still alive, but even if he is, he would be much older than Mr. Jivaro."

"Mr. who?" Miss Nash asked loudly, trying to make herself heard over the cries of some nearby passengers.

"Anton Jivaro is the hijacker's real name," Frank explained. "He's an escaped mental patient my dad's been trying to track down."

"What!" she exlaimed. "You mean we're in the hands of a madman?"

Just then the cockpit door opened and the hijacker and flight attendant emerged. The frightened burst of conversation that had broken out throughout the plane suddenly died.

A slightly shaken voice came over the intercom. "This is your captain. As you all know, the plane has been hijacked. Please stay calm. The hijacker has promised not to harm anyone if we all do as he says. He tells me he is the Maharaja of Kashmir. I don't want any heroes attempting to subdue him, because he is carrying dynamite. My instructions are to change course from Los Angeles to Miami. There we will refuel to fly, via Casablanca, to Kashmir. We are now on the way to Miami."

The hijacker spoke up. "All of you are to obey the captain and stay calm. We'll carry on just as though eveything was normal." He turned to the flight attendant. "Isn't it about time you served lunch?"

"Lunch?" she said, flustered. "Oh, yes. Ladies and gentlemen, we will now have lunch."

The strain of being in great danger left few of the passengers hungry, and some were so upset that they could not eat at all. The Hardys only picked at their food, and even Chet's appetite was diminished. Only the hijacker ate with gusto, standing at the rear of the plane.

Shortly after the meal, the captain's voice came over the intercom again. "Ground Control at Miami reports the airport closed in by fog," he announced. "Will the maharaja please come forward to discuss an alternate landing place?"

Jivaro walked up to the flight attendant. "Go tell him to make an instrument landing."

The young woman disappeared into the cockpit. When she came out a few moments later, she called to the hijacker. "The skipper wants to see you."

Jivaro moved forward, but when the flight attendant opened the door to the cockpit for him, he shook his head. "I want my eye on the passengers," he said. "We'll talk through the door."

The voice of the captain was heard. "It's too

dangerous to land at Miami, Maharaja. The south Atlantic and Gulf coasts are socked in by fog clear to Mobile. Ground Control recommends New Orleans."

"We will land at Miami," the hijacker insisted. "Unless you want to land right now, in pieces."

"Can't we talk about it?"

"No. You have instruments to land in a fog. Use them."

The captain sighed. "Close the door, Peg," he said to the flight attendant.

Jivaro returned to his position at the rear of the plane. Again the captain's voice came over the intercom.

"Ladies and gentlemen, in case some of you couldn't hear my conversation with the maharaja, we are going down at Miami despite the fog condition there. We will be landing in about one hour. Please don't be alarmed. We are equipped with instruments for a blind landing. While not quite as safe as visual landing, we'll make it. However, we will take certain routine precautions so you're not shaken up too much in case it gets a little rough. The flight attendant will instruct you."

Raising her voice, Peg said, "Please remove all sharp objects from your pockets. Women passengers should take off shoes with high heels. When the seat belt light goes on, fasten your belt loosely enough so that you can bend forward with your head between your knees, and cover your head with your hands."

With frightened expressions on their faces, the passengers followed her instructions. Nervously, Vern asked Joe in a low voice, "How safe is a blind landing?"

"Not very," Joe muttered. "The captain was just trying to prevent panic. If he comes in a few feet too low, we'll belly flop and skid maybe a quarter mile. The friction could set the plane on fire. If he comes in a few feet too high, we could hit the control tower."

Frank added reassuringly, "But on the other hand, instrument landings are often made without even shaking up the passengers."

An hour later, the "Fasten Seat Belts" sign went on, and the captain could be heard on the intercom. "We will be landing in five minutes. Please follow the instructions given you."

The passengers fastened their seat belts loosely, leaned forward, and gripped their heads between their knees with both hands. The hijacker took an empty seat in the back of the plane, and leaned into the aisle so that he could keep an eye on everyone. The cadence of the engines changed as the plane dropped. Suddenly, the wheels struck the ground hard. The plane bounced, came down again, and taxied smoothly along the runway.

Cries of relief filled the cabin. A few sobs were heard, and Chet looked so white that Frank was afraid his friend would pass out.

When the plane stopped, everyone got up and looked through the windows. Outside there was a blank wall of fog.

The captain said over the intercom, "All right, Maharaja, we're down. Now what?"

The hijacker, back on his feet, moved forward to open the cockpit door. Without going inside, he asked, "Do police have the plane surrounded?"

"I imagine so," the captain replied. "Do you want to talk to them?"

"No, I merely want them to keep their distance. Order the plane refueled."

"This plane isn't designed for overseas flight, Maharaja," the captain pointed out. "But we could make Casablanca with less weight. If you'd release the passengers and just keep the crew, we'd be better off."

After considering, Jivaro gave in. "All right, I'll let most of them go, and just keep five. It would lighten the plane even more to unload the baggage, so have that done, too. But no tricks. If any cops come aboard as baggage handlers, I'll blow us all up."

"They couldn't," the captain said. "There's only an outside door to the baggage compartment, and no way to get in here from there."

"All right. Have the stuff removed and the plane refueled. When that's finished, I'll release everyone but five hostages."

Some time passed before the captain announced that the plane was refueled and they were ready to take off.

Satisfied that everything had been carried out as he had requested, the hijacker walked back to the center of the plane and pointed to the Hardy boys, Vern, Chet, and Cylvia Nash. "You five stay aboard. Everyone else can get off."

As the passengers were leaving, Jivaro said to Frank and Joe, "I warned your father to get off my back. Because he didn't, you two are going to end up in Kashmir."

When everyone but the hostages and the crew were off the plane, Joe got to his feet and stepped past Frank into the aisle.

"What's on your mind?" the hijacker hissed.

"I don't think you'd blow up this plane, because you'd have to blow yourself up, too."

Opening his coat, Jivaro gripped the loop on the end of the lanyard. "Test me," he challenged.

After studying the six tubes strapped to the man's body, Joe suddenly grabbed him and threw him down into the aisle! The hijacker jerked the lanyard, and Cylvia Nash screamed in terror!

4 A Clever Escape

Frantically, the hostages and the crew dived behind seats in a desperate attempt to escape the explosion. But nothing happened!

As Joe fell on top of the hijacker, the little man squirmed like an eel from his grip and delivered a karate chop to Joe's neck that momentarily stunned the boy. Then Jivaro jumped to his feet and raced for the emergency exit. By the time the others cautiously peeked above the headrests, the fake maharaja had opened the emergency door. He slipped through it, letting himself down by his hands, and dropped the dozen feet or so to the ground.

Frank rushed after him to the door, but he could see nothing through the thick blanket of fog.

Meanwhile, the flight attendant ran to the cockpit and returned with the pilot, the copilot, and the navigator. When the captain, a large, ruddy-faced man, learned what had happened, he hurried back to the cockpit to radio the surrounding police.

By then Joe had recovered from the karate chop. Frank asked him why he had taken the chance of jumping the hijacker.

"I recognized his so-called dynamite as highway flares," Joe told him. "It was all a bluff!"

Police, led by a uniformed lieutenant, raced aboard the plane. After questioning the witnesses about the hijacker's escape, the lieutenant ordered the entire landing field sealed off and searched.

At once, his men left to put the order into effect, and the lieutenant turned to the flight attendant. "I suppose he gave a fake name, but how was this kook listed on the manifest?"

She went to get her clipboard. "John Smith," she reported.

"Figures," the lieutenant said glumly.

"His real name is Anton Jivaro," Frank volunteered.

The lieutenant looked at him in surprise. "Who are you?"

"Frank Hardy." He pointed to his companions. "This is my brother Joe and my friends, Chet Morton and Vern Nelson."

Nodding acknowledgment, the lieutenant asked, "How do you happen to know this screwball's name?"

"My father's been trying to hunt him down," Frank said. "He's an escaped mental patient."

"Who is your father?"

"Fenton Hardy."

The lieutenant looked impressed. "I've heard a lot about him. So you two are the famous Hardy boys."

"We're the Hardy boys," Joe said modestly. "I don't know about famous."

The lieutenant grinned. "Give me a description of Anton Jivaro," he said.

The boys told all they knew about the fake maharaja while the lieutenant made notes. Just then, a police sergeant returned to report that no trace of the hijacker had been found.

"The fog is so thick, he could easily have sneaked by the cordon," the officer said. "I'm having the terminal and hangars searched right now."

"Also put out an all-points bulletin," the lieutenant instructed. "The man's name is Anton Jivaro." He rattled off a description from his notes.

"Yes, sir," the sergeant said, and left again.

The lieutenant turned to the captain, "You may as well reload your passengers and continue to Los Angeles."

Even though the plane was already refueled, it took some time before it could start again. The passengers, who had not yet recovered from their fright, boarded reluctantly, and all the luggage had to be reloaded.

Shortly after they were airborne, Chet said, "I just thought of where that hijacker might be."

"Where?" Frank asked.

"In the baggage compartment!"

"Oh, my!" Cylvia Nash said. "You mean he could hijack us again?"

"No. There's no way to get from the baggage compartment into the cabin while we're in flight," Frank said reassuringly. "Didn't you hear the captain say that? Besides, Chet's brainstorms are usually not on target."

"I figured it out logically," Chet insisted. "In the fog the hijacker could have hidden under the plane, or maybe in one of the wheel housings. I read about a young boy stowing away in a wheel housing once. While the stuff was being reloaded, Jivaro could have climbed through the open door."

"Two things wrong with that," Joe said. "The door's too high above the ground, and the baggage handlers would have seen him."

"Not so," Chet said. "It's a low opening at the back of the plane, not up high like the passenger entrance. And the handlers had to make more than one trip to load all those suitcases. They wouldn't close the door between trips. He could have gotten aboard easily."

"Could he survive in there?" Vern asked. "I mean, is the baggage compartment pressurized?"

"Sure," Chet said. "They ship pets in there, don't they?"

"Well, there's no way to check now," Frank said. "You can't get into the compartment from here any more than Jivaro could get into the cabin."

The flight to California was uneventful. Chet checked the rest of his nickels, but found none of any real value. The others tried to relax, and Cylvia closed her eyes in a futile attempt to take a nap. At ten P.M. they landed at Los Angeles International Airport.

As the boys were starting to debark, a baggage truck manned by two handlers backed up to the plane and one of them unlatched the baggage compartment door. As they pulled it open, a small, dark figure suddenly dashed out, knocking the men down as he pushed past them.

Before the dazed baggage handlers realized what had happened, the hijacker jumped from the truck and raced off across the field toward a distant chain-link fence.

Joe had watched Jivaro's swift escape and ran down the gangway as fast as he could. "Chet was right!" he exclaimed. "Let's get him!"

The four boys rushed after the fugitive. However, the hijacker had gained too much of a lead. Reaching the fence twenty yards ahead of them, he climbed up and over it with the agility of a monkey. He dashed to the corner and hopped aboard a bus that had just stopped.

Frank and Joe started to scale the fence, but dropped to the ground when the bus pulled away. Grimly, they walked back to the plane which by now was swarming with security guards who were questioning the passengers. Cylvia Nash pointed to the young detectives excitedly. "Here are the boys who chased after the man when he jumped out," she said.

The chief security guard turned to the Hardys. "Was it the hijacker Miami wired us about?" he asked.

"Yes," Frank replied. "He climbed over the fence and caught a bus at the corner."

"We'll try to have that bus stopped," the security officer said, and immediately began talking into his walkie-talkie.

The passengers were finally allowed to leave, and the four boys found themselves behind Cylvia when they entered the terminal. She quickened her pace and was warmly greeted by a lanky, red-haired man waiting for her.

Joe watched the two curiously. "I've seen this guy somewhere before," he mused.

The other three turned to observe the man.

"No wonder he looks familiar!" Vern exclaimed. "I think that's the man who stole my car!"

The lanky redhead was now walking next to Cylvia, so that his back was turned to them. But the boys had gotten a good look at him.

"I'm sure it is," Chet confirmed. "Didn't Mr. Hardy say his name was Red Sluice?"

"That's right," Joe said. "Let's grab him."

"We can't," Frank demurred. "We have no proof. Let's follow him instead. You go get our luggage. I'll rent a car and pull up outside."

He hurried across the lobby to a rental desk while the other three headed for the baggage area. The rental cars were parked in a lot across the street. Frank got a four-door sedan and was waiting for the boys when they came out of the terminal carrying their suitcases.

"Miss Nash's luggage hasn't come down the chute yet," Joe said as they loaded their bags in the trunk. "We've got plenty of time."

33

He climbed in front next to Frank, while Vern and Chet settled in the back. Soon Miss Nash and Red Sluice emerged, the latter carrying a large suitcase. They crossed the street to the public parking lot.

"The exit is right there," Joe said, pointing ahead. "So we're in a good position to take up the chase."

In a few minutes, the red-haired man and Miss Nash drove off in a red sports car with its top down.

"That ought to be easy to tail," Frank said, shifting into gear.

Sluice took the San Diego Freeway north to the Ventura Freeway, then east a short distance to the Hollywood Freeway. Turning into downtown Los Angeles, he pulled up in front of an apartment house on Parkview, directly across from Douglas MacArthur Park. Frank parked a quarter of a block away, and quietly they watched Red Sluice follow Cylvia Nash into the building.

As they disappeared, Joe slipped from the car. "I'll go after them," he volunteered, and walked to the front entrance of the apartment house. He went in and almost immediately came out again.

As he climbed back into the car, he said, "Her name's listed in the lobby, Apartment 2B. Now what do we do?"

"Wait," Frank said.

Five minutes later, Red Sluice left the building.

He climbed into the sports car and drove off. Frank followed. The lanky redhead led them to a small house a dozen blocks away. He pulled into an open carport attached to the house, then went inside.

Frank again parked a quarter of a block away on the opposite side of the street, where there was no light.

"What now?" Joe asked.

"We'll wait a while to see if he comes out again to lead us somewhere else," Frank said.

"You know it's almost eleven?" Chet inquired.

"So?" Frank asked.

"That makes it two A.M. in Bayport. I'm getting sleepy."

"If nothing happens in fifteen minutes, we'll find a hotel," Frank promised.

Just then a small, furtive-looking man came into view on the opposite side of the street. As he passed beneath a light, Joe stiffened. "That's Anton Jivaro!" he blurted out.

The hijacker turned toward the house Red Sluice had entered. With bated breath, the boys watched him ring the doorbell!

5 The Plant

The door opened and Jivaro entered.

"Joe and I'll do a little spying," Frank said tensely, turning to Chet. "You and Vern stay here. You'd better get behind the wheel so we can take off fast if we run into trouble."

"Okay."

The Hardys got out of the car, crossed the street, and walked up to the house. They could not see into the front room because the drapes were drawn. Tiptoeing to the door, they listened, but heard nothing.

"You check to the left, and I'll go to the right," Frank whispered to his brother.

Joe nodded, and the two separated. There were

lights behind drawn drapes in windows on both sides, but they could not see in or hear anything. They met in the back, where all was dark.

"Any luck?" Frank asked in a low voice.

"No," Joe replied.

At that moment, a kitchen light went on and they noticed that the screened window was open. Tiptoeing over, they peered inside. Anton Jivaro was seating himself at the table, while Red Sluice turned on the gas under a kettle.

"All I got is instant," the lanky redhead said.

"It's all right," the hijacker told him.

Sluice put his hands on his hips and regarded the little man dourly. "If you weren't an old partner of mine, I'd turn you in. Course you're doing a good job of that yourself by making headlines all over the world with that silly hijack attempt. With all that publicity, you're easy to trace."

"I was just trying to collect my inheritance," Jivaro said sullenly.

"What inheritance? Will you get over the crazy idea that you're a maharaja?"

"But I am. My father was the son of Kashmir's last monarch, Maharaja Hari Singh."

"Your father was a used car salesman in Brooklyn."

"Just because he was a car salesman doesn't mean he wasn't the maharaja's son," Jivaro argued. "There are ex-kings working as waiters in New York

37

City. My grandfather went into exile and passed away twelve years later, making my father next in line. When he died, I became maharaja."

"I looked up Kashmir at the library," Red said impatiently. "The last maharaja's only son was Dr. Karan Singh, who was elected president after his father was deposed. You've got to stop telling people you're a maharaja."

The kettle whistled and Red made two cups of instant coffee. Then he sat down across the table from his old partner.

"What are your plans now?" he asked.

"I figured you'd put me to work at your plant."

"You're even crazier than I thought! You think I'm going to risk the whole operation by bringing a looney into the gang? I don't know what happened to you, but as long as you don't know your name, you can't work with me!"

"Would you rather I tipped off the cops to who robbed that bank in Boston?"

Red Sluice's eyes narrowed. "Blackmail?"

"Let's say you're going to hire me only because we go back a long time," the little man suggested.

After a period of silence, Red chuckled grimly. "Well, I guess we both have something on each other, then. All right, you can start in the morning. But you got to promise you'll forget this maharaja stuff."

"I won't tell anybody who I really am," Anton Jivaro agreed.

"Okay, we'll be leaving at eight, so we better get to bed as soon as we finish our coffee."

There was a meow right next to Frank and Joe, and both boys turned in the direction of the sound. A cat stood at the back door. While they stared at the feline, Red Sluice rose and opened the door. "Okay, kitty, come on in," he said, then spotted the two boys.

"Who are you?" he yelled, rushing at them.

Frank and Joe ducked around the corner of the house and ran off, with Sluice right behind them. Chet saw them coming and started the engine. Vern, who had moved into the front with Chet, leaned over and opened the right rear door. Frank and Joe dived into the car, and Chet gunned away so fast that the door slammed shut by itself.

The Hardys looked back to see Red Sluice standing in the street, shaking his fist.

"What happened?" Chet asked as he slowed to round a corner.

"He caught us listening at a window," Frank said.

"Did you find out anything?" Vern inquired.

"Sure did," Frank replied, and related what they had heard. "We'll come back in the morning to follow them to the plant Red Sluice mentioned," he added.

They went to a downtown hotel, where they got connecting rooms with twin beds. By now it was after midnight, and the boys went to sleep instantly.

The next morning they had a quick breakfast, then drove to Red Sluice's house. By seven-thirty, they were parked across the street. At eight, the lanky redhead and Jivaro came out and climbed into the red sports car. When they drove off, the gray sedan followed.

Frank, who was behind the wheel, kept a safe distance as the thief led them to a warehouse at the edge of Old Chinatown. Sluice parked in front, while Frank drove past and stopped a hundred feet away. Through the rear window, the boys watched Red and Anton Jivaro enter the warehouse.

Frank drove around the block and turned into an alley in back of the building. He told Chet to get behind the wheel while he and Joe investigated the warehouse.

There was a large sliding door at the rear of the building that was locked from inside. Next to it was a window about four feet from the ground. It was too dirty to see through, but Frank wiped clean a circular area with a scrap of newspaper he found and peered into a restroom.

"See if we can get in through the window," Joe urged.

Frank nodded and pushed up the lower part.

40

Since the room was empty, the two boys climbed over the sill, letting themselves down carefully on the other side. They tiptoed to the door across from the window, opened it a crack, and peered out into a large, barnlike room. It contained about twenty new and almost new cars! A dozen men in coveralls were working on them, systematically taking them apart.

"Why are they doing this?" Joe whispered.

"It must be for spare parts," Frank whispered back. "Remember Dad guessed they were either repainting the cars, or stripping them for parts to sell on the black market."

"Do you see Red and his crazy friend?" Joe asked.

Frank shook his head. "No one's looking this way. Let's poke around a little."

He eased the door open enough for them to slip through. Quickly they ducked behind a partially dismantled car and glanced around. They noticed a door centered in the wall to their right, and another open one on the left which led into a small office. Red Sluice and Anton Jivaro were inside. Apparently, Red was introducing Jivaro to the burly man behind a large oak desk.

"That big guy must be the boss of the operation," Joe whispered.

"Probably just the boss of the warehouse," Frank replied. "Dad said the tattooed guy named Crafty

41

Kraft was one of the ring's chief lieutenants, so he's probably in charge of the car thefts."

A man crossed over to the door in the right wall, opened it, and went through. A moment later, he returned carrying a wrench, closed the door behind him, and went back to work.

"Let's see what's in that room," Frank suggested.

"Right in front of those workmen?" Joe objected.

"With all the people around here, no one's going to notice. Where's your spirit of adventure?"

Joe shrugged. "I'm game if you are."

No one glanced their way as the Hardys casually sauntered over to the closed door. Frank opened it a few inches and peered into the room to make sure it was empty. Then the boys slipped inside and Frank shut the door behind them.

It was a small machine shop, containing a metal lathe, a planer, a drill press, and a number of other power tools. Hanging from the walls were assorted hand tools, such as wrenches and screwdrivers.

"They must use these to fix up the spare parts so they look like new," Joe surmised.

"Probably," Frank agreed.

"Well, let's get out of here before someone else comes for a tool."

But Joe's advice was too late. At that moment another workman came in. He was tall, thin, and had a bald head. When he saw the boys, he raised the large wrench he was carrying like a weapon.

"What are you doing here?" he hissed. "You don't belong in this place!"

6 Caught!

Frank and Joe regarded the raised wrench warily.

"I said what are you doing here?" the workman repeated.

"We, eh, we're looking for jobs," Joe replied, hoping he could talk his way out of the situation. "The front door was locked and nobody answered, so we came in the back way. We thought this was the hiring office, but I guess it isn't."

The workman looked them over suspiciously. "What made you think we needed help?"

"We're auto mechanics," Frank put in. "Isn't this a repair shop?"

Another workman stepped into the room, and

came to a halt when he saw the baldheaded man holding the boys at bay with his wrench.

"What's going on?" he inquired.

"I caught these two nosing around. They claim they're looking for jobs and wandered in here because they thought it was the hiring office."

"Wandered in how? Both the front and back doors are locked!"

"The back door was open," Joe said, his heart pounding.

"What do you think?" the baldheaded man asked his companion.

"We better take them over to the office and let Big Harry handle it."

"Okay, you two," the man with the wrench ordered, gesturing toward the door. "March!"

Frank and Joe had no choice but to obey. They were herded across the big garage to the office on its opposite side. On the way, they saw Red Sluice and Anton Jivaro standing toward the front of the building with their backs turned, talking to one of the mechanics.

In the office, the burly man behind the desk looked up in surprise as the boys were shoved in by the two workmen.

"What's this, Slim?" he asked the baldheaded man.

"I found these two in the machine shop. They

claim they were looking for work and thought that was the hiring office."

Frowning at the boys, Big Harry asked, "How'd you get in here?"

"The back door was open," Joe said.

"Who left it unlocked?" Harry demanded in an accusing voice.

"Not me," Slim said. "I wasn't the last one in. Anyway, I think they're lying."

"Bruce, go check the door," Big Harry ordered the other workman.

Frank said, "It fell shut behind us. It might have locked itself."

Bruce paused in the doorway, looking at his employer inquiringly.

"Never mind," Big Harry said impatiently. He stared at the two boys. "What's your names?"

"I'm Joe Bayport," Joe said. "He's my brother Frank."

Just then Red Sluice walked into the office, took one look at the boys and exclaimed, "What are you two doing here?"

"You know them?" Big Harry asked.

"I sure do!"

"Slim and Bruce found them lurking around the machine shop. Who are they?"

"I don't know their names, but they were hanging around my house last night also. They were peeking

46

in a window, getting ready to break in I think," Red explained.

"You sure they're the same ones?" Big Harry asked.

"Positive. Anton and I were having coffee in the kitchen when the cat meowed to get in. I opened the door and saw them because the light from the kitchen window was shining right in their faces."

"To make sure, go get your old friend," Big Harry suggested.

With sinking hearts, Frank and Joe realized that once Jivaro saw them, he would recognize them as the Hardy boys. As long as the crooks thought they were just thieves, they had a good chance of being let go with just a lecture. But if it was discovered they they were the sons of the private detective investigating the car-theft ring, they were in big trouble!

But Red Sluice gave them a brief respite. "My friend didn't see them," he admitted. They got away before he came out. I chased them until they jumped into a car and drove off."

"Okay, boys," Big Harry said to Frank and Joe. "Get out your I.D.s."

The boys winced inwardly. This was just as bad as being identified by Jivaro. Desperately, Joe stalled by saying, "I'm not carrying any."

"Neither am I," Frank added.

47

"Search them for wallets," Big Harry ordered.

Joe had kept an eye on the man with the wrench. When Slim let it hang at his side, feeling the boys would not try a break, the young detective suddenly reached out and grabbed it from his hand.

Tossing it into a wastebasket across the room, he yelled, "Come on, Frank!" and headed for the door.

Slim stepped in front of him, though, and delivered a roundhouse right. Joe ducked under it, drove a fist into the man's belly, then delivered an uppercut that sent his opponent reeling backwards.

Red Sluice swung at Frank, who ducked the blow. An instant later, Bruce knocked Frank down with a hard right to the jaw. But as he bore in to finish the boy off, Joe stuck out a foot to trip him. A moment later, Bruce was flat on his face.

As Frank recovered, Red Sluice rushed at him. Frank pushed him back into Big Harry, who had just come around the desk to join in the fray.

As the two workmen again moved in for the attack, Joe shoved Slim, Frank hit Bruce, and the two men crashed together, going down with a loud thud.

"Let's get out of here!" Joe yelled, leading the way through the door.

They were almost to the restroom when the four hoods recovered sufficiently to run after them. The boys darted inside and Frank slammed and bolted the door. They climbed out the window just as a heavy shoulder hit the door from the other side.

Chet started the engine and Vern leaned over to let the Hardys into the rear of the car. When Chet pulled away, the back door of the warehouse opened and the four hoods rushed out.

"After them!" Big Harry yelled.

Looking through the rear window, the boys saw the thieves jump into a green sedan parked behind the warehouse. Big Harry took the wheel, swung around, and raced after them.

Chet sped down an alley and turned right at the cross street before the other car came in sight behind them. Then he swung left into another alley. He continued this winding course for some blocks until he was sure they had shaken their pursuers.

"Now what?" he asked. "Back to the hotel?"

"May as well," Frank said.

Chet continued on for a few minutes, then pulled over to the curb. "Which way is it?"

"Are you lost?" Vern inquired.

"No, but I think the car is!" he joked, relieving the tension.

The four boys laughed and then looked carefully in all directions. Chet's winding course had confused everyone.

"I think it's that way," Joe said, pointing.

Chet started up again, but after a few minutes,

they realized they were driving deeper and deeper into Old Chinatown. The streets became narrow and buildings on both sides pushed right up to the sidewalks.

Glancing into the rearview mirror, Chet suddenly said. "Uh-oh."

The others turned around to look. A block behind them, the hoods had just turned a corner. Apparently, they had been randomly cruising side streets in search of the boys and had finally sighted them.

Chet turned right, then swung left into an alley, attempting the same zigzag maneuver as before. But the other car was too close behind this time. It followed wherever the boys went.

As they sped along one of the narrow streets, Chet sighed. "Hey, here's a whole block of Chinese restaurants."

"Want to stop for a snack?" Vern inquired sarcastically. Chet did not reply.

They went past a sign reading ROAD CONSTRUCTION AHEAD, and the pavement suddenly became slick with mud spewed up from a drainage ditch being dug to their right. On their left, a flimsy wooden guard rail edged a sheer twenty-foot drop into a rocky ditch.

The pursuing car put on a burst of speed and began to come up alongside the boys.

"They're going to run you into the ditch, Chet!"

Frank cautioned. "Give them a driving lesson."

Chet nodded and suddenly slammed on his brakes. He let the green sedan shoot past, then swung left, and gently prodded their opponents' bumper. Accelerating, he nudged the hoods' car forward and sideways so that they, instead of the boys, nosed over toward the ditch.

Finally, the green sedan came to a halt with its radiator buried in the mudbank. Chet swung back to the right in order to straighten his wheel. Just then he hit a patch of mud, skidded, and headed directly for the guard rail with the twenty-foot vertical drop beyond!

7 The Stakeout

Chet turned the front wheels into the direction of the skid. The car veered sidewise, but straightened out just as the left rear fender scraped the guard rail. Gritting his teeth, Chet fought for control, and was finally able to drive onto the right side of the road.

"Whew!" Vern muttered. "Was everybody as scared as I was?"

"I wasn't scared at all," Chet said, his voice shaking. "I've got nerves of steel." Then, exhausted, he slumped behind the wheel, resting his head against the window. Frank twisted in his seat to see what happened to the green sedan. Big Harry and

Red Sluice were angrily trying to push the car out of the ditch, but the harder they struggled the more embedded the vehicle became.

All four boys chuckled smugly, but not wanting to push their luck, they drove quickly back to the hotel, where they decided to phone Fenton Hardy in Bayport.

Frank dialed and Gertrude Hardy answered.

"Are you all right?" she asked anxiously. "We heard on TV about that terrible hijacking."

"We're all fine, Aunt Gertrude. Is Dad there?"

"No, he's gone away. He said it was a secret mission. You're to leave word where you can be reached, and he'll get in touch with you."

Frank gave her the telephone number of the hotel and their room numbers.

"Have you found Vern's nickel?" Aunt Gertrude asked.

"We haven't had time to look yet," Frank said. "Maybe we'll get to it this afternoon."

"All right. I'm glad that this time it's just a simple mystery, and you're not involved with criminals."

"Yes, Aunt Gertrude. Say hello to Mom."

When Frank hung up, Joe raised his eyebrows. "Dad isn't there?"

"No. He's on some kind of secret mission. I wish we'd been able to talk to him, so we could discuss our next move."

"That's simple," Chet said. "We call the police and tell them about that warehouse."

"That may not be a good idea just yet. If they raid the place, all they'll get is the small fry. We want the kingpin of the operation!"

"Maybe it's Big Harry," Chet said.

"I doubt it."

"So how do we get the chief?" Vern asked.

"We could stake the place out and photograph everyone who goes in or out with our pocket cameras," Joe suggested.

"Good idea," Frank agreed. "The big boss is bound to show up eventually and when he does, we'll have some real evidence to turn over to the police."

All four agreed that this was the best plan. They decided to watch the warehouse in shifts. Frank and Chet were to take the first one, while Joe and Vern would check up on the Liberty Head nickel. They all drove to the warehouse and parked a block away. Getting out of the car, the boys scouted the area.

No one was in sight as they approached the front of the building. A number of empty wooden crates and cardboard boxes were piled near the entrance. While the others kept watch, Frank picked out a large shipping carton that had contained a refrigerator. He used his pocketknife to make a door in the back of it, cutting only the top, bottom, and left side, and then bent the right side so that the door could be opened and closed. He set a small wooden crate into the carton to serve as a seat, then put a hole at eye level.

"This'll make a great 'guard house' for me in front," he declared, turning to his friends. "Now let's find a place for Chet to hide in back of the building."

They began walking toward the alley to pick a safe spot when suddenly Frank, who was in the lead, motioned for everyone to move out of sight. Big Harry was parking behind the warehouse. The sedan's radiator was caked with dried mud, but none of the occupants seemed to have been injured in the accident. They all got out and went into the building.

Frank watched them, gingerly peeking around the corner.

"What's going on?" Joe whispered.

"Nothing now," Frank said. He moved forward and motioned for the others to follow him. "The hoods who chased us just got back and went inside. None of them seemed to be hurt."

As they neared the sedan, Vern said, "Those guys must have had a tow truck rescue them. They couldn't have backed out on their own. They were nose-first in that mud bank."

There was a small shed right across from the rear

door of the warehouse on the other side of the alley. They found it unlocked and went in. It was empty. A dirt-encrusted window faced the building. When Chet scraped clean a spot about the size of a silver dollar, he had a perfect view of the door.

Handing him his pocket camera, Joe said, "Snap pictures of everyone going in or out. Okay?"

"When are you guys coming to relieve us?" Chet asked.

"Soon as Vern and I finish our business," Joe told him. "Shouldn't be later than one o'clock."

"You mean we have to wait until then for lunch?"

"It's not going to hurt you," Vern chided him.

Chet grimaced. "You skinny guys can talk, but it takes sustenance to maintain a muscular body like mine!"

"Oh sure, real muscular!" Vern teased his cousin, as he and the Hardys started back to the street. Frank quickly took up his station in the refrigerator carton, while Joe and Vern went back to the car.

Slipping behind the wheel, Joe asked, "Where to?"

"First, we ought to see the lawyer in charge of Uncle Gregg's estate," Vern suggested. "He's in the Nichols Building downtown. His name is Charles Avery."

The attorney had a plush office on the seventeenth floor. He was a plump, middle-aged, cheerful-looking man. Greeting the boys courteously, he asked them to sit down in comfortable chairs.

"As you know, your uncle had severe financial reverses shortly before he died," the lawyer told Vern. "Even his extensive coin collection had to be sold to satisfy claims against the estate. All, that is, but the 1913 Liberty Head nickel, which he left to you. Unfortunately, that has disappeared."

"How?" Vern asked.

"The president of the bank where your uncle had his safe-deposit box can explain that," Charles Avery said. "Let me phone Mr. Barton Laing of the Bunker Bank to make an appointment for you."

The lawyer called and was able to arrange an immediate meeting between Mr. Laing and the boys.

The bank was only two blocks from the Nichols Building, so they left their car where they had parked it and walked. Barton Laing, a tall, slightly stooped man with gray hair, shook hands with the boys and invited them into his office. When all three were seated, he leaned back in his desk chair and began folding and unfolding his hands.

"This is quite embarrassing to the bank, Mr. Nelson," he said to Vern nervously. "Of course, we have no legal responsibility for the missing coin. The only evidence that it was ever in your uncle's safe-deposit box is a statement in his will that on a particular date he placed it there. Nobody saw him do it, because what customers put in or take out of their boxes is their private business."

"Why would he say he put it there if he didn't?" Vern asked.

"I can't imagine."

Joe spoke up. "Could he have taken it out again and not changed his will?"

The banker shook his head. "He never opened the box after the day he deposited it."

"How can you be sure of that?" Vern asked.

"Our records show every visit. Whenever a customer uses his safe-deposit box, he must sign a card giving not only the date, but the exact time of day. Our files show no such visits after the date specified in his will."

"Could a bank employee have gotten into the box?" Joe asked.

Mr. Laing frowned. "Impossible. No one but the boxholder possesses a key. A boxholder's key, that is. There is, of course, the bank's master key."

"Master key?" Vern repeated.

"Let me explain the procedure. It takes two keys to open a box, the customer's and the bank's. The bank key fits all boxes. But it can't open a box by itself. The customer's key must be used along with it."

Vern said, "Then when Uncle Gregg put the coin in the box, somebody saw him do it."

"Not necessarily. Usual procedure is for the customer to carry his box into one of the curtained alcoves in the vault room, where he can transact his business in privacy. When he's ready to return the box, he calls the vault clerk, who uses both keys to lock it up again."

Joe spoke up. "But if Mr. Nelson had chosen not to use a private alcove, he could have put the coin into his box right in front of the vault clerk, couldn't he?"

"Oh yes, but there would be no record of whether or not he did that."

"Would there be a record of who the vault clerk was that day?"

"Of course. She signs the card."

"Has she been asked whether or not she saw Mr. Nelson put the coin into the box?"

Barton Laing gave Joe an indulgent smile. "It's hardly likely an employee would recall anything about a transaction that took place so many years ago. The person on vault duty may usher as many as fifty people to their safe-deposit boxes in a single day."

"Is the clerk still employed here?"

"I have no idea," Mr. Laing said. "But I'll find out."

59

Picking up his desk phone, he asked for the safe-deposit-box records to be brought to his office. A few minutes later, a young man delivered a metal file-card holder.

"Want me to wait?" he asked.

The bank president shook his head. "You can pick it up later."

As the clerk left, Mr. Laing began thumbing through the cards. Finally, he pulled one out.

"Here it is," he said. "Yes, she's still working here."

"Let's ask her if she remembers Mr. Nelson using his box that day," Joe suggested.

Shrugging, the banker again picked up his phone. "I doubt that she'll remember, but we'll try." Into the phone he said, "Send in the vault clerk, please."

After a few moments' wait, there was a knock on the office door.

"Come in," Barton Laing called.

The door opened and the boys gaped. Cylvia Nash stepped into the room!

8 Trapped!

"Why, hello, boys," Cylvia said in surprise. "What are you doing here?"

"You know these two?" Barton Laing asked.

"They were on the plane with me," she explained. "In fact Joe was the one who nearly captured the hijacker."

"They want to talk to you about Gregg Nelson's missing coin," the bank president said.

"Oh, are you the nephew?" Cylvia asked Vern. "That never occurred to me when we met."

Vern grinned. "It's a common name."

"Miss Nash," Barton Laing said, "You're registered as the one who admitted Mr. Nelson to the

61

vault eight years ago when, according to his will, he put the coin in his safe-deposit box. Do you remember that day?"

"So long ago?" She shook her head.

"No recollection at all of seeing the coin?" Joe asked.

"I don't even remember signing Mr. Nelson in."

Mr. Laing shrugged. "I guess that settles that," he said. "Sorry."

"It's not your fault," Vern smiled wryly. "And after all, it's only a hundred thousand dollars."

As the boys walked back to the car, Joe said, "I might believe Miss Nash if we hadn't seen who met her at the airport. But people who associate with crooks are usually crooked too. For all we know, she was the one who stole your uncle's coin!"

"I don't see any way to find out," Vern said.

"Don't give up so easily," Joe advised. "We know where she lives. Maybe there's some evidence at her apartment."

"Well, we can't just break in!"

"Of course not. But I have a plan. Let's buy some coveralls."

Joe drove to a department store, where each bought a suit of work clothes. Next, they went to a hardware store and bought tool belts resembling those worn by telephone repairmen. They returned to the hotel long enough to change into their outfits and then drove to Cylvia's home.

They parked in front of the building, went inside, and rang the apartment manager's bell.

An elderly woman answered the door. Joe smiled. "Telephone company, ma'am. The tenant in 2B reported her phone out of order."

"She isn't at home days," the woman said. "I'll have to let you in."

Leading the way up to the second floor, the manager opened the door of 2B with a passkey.

"Set the lock when you come out," she told them.

"Yes, ma'am," Joe promised.

At the warehouse, meanwhile, Chet was getting tired of peering through the small clean spot in the dirt-encrusted window. He was also getting hungry, thinking about hot dogs, hamburgers, and pizza.

Just then, he saw a small Chinese boy about four years old meander by, clutching a dollar bill in his hand. A few minutes later the child came back, working a yo-yo with his right hand and licking an ice-cream bar on a stick in his left. Chet could not stand it any longer. He ran out the door and after the boy.

"Hey, kid," he called out.

The child stopped to regard him with large eyes.

Chet took out a dollar bill. "Do me a favor and I'll give you a quarter. Go back to where you got the ice cream and get me one, too."

"Eh?" the child said.

When Chet repeated himself, the little boy answered in a stream of Cantonese.

"Don't speak English, huh?" Chet said. He pointed at the bar, then down the alley in the direction of a delicatessen he'd seen earlier.

Smiling, the child held his ice cream up toward Chet's mouth.

"No, I don't want a lick," Chet said. "I want a whole one." Again gesturing in the direction of the delicatessen, he held out the dollar bill.

The little boy suddenly looked as though he understood. Smiling broadly and nodding his head, he accepted the bill.

He turned around and retraced his way toward the store while Chet slipped into the shed again and put his eye back to the peephole.

When he spotted the little boy on his way back, he hurried out into the alley. With a big smile, the child handed him a yo-yo and a quarter in change, spouted a friendly stream of Cantonese, and walked away. Chet stared after him darkly, his stomach rumbling.

Out in front, Frank was getting just as tired of

sitting in the refrigerator carton. His interest perked up when the warehouse door opened and Red Sluice came out with Anton Jivaro. The red sports car was parked only a few feet from Frank's box, and he could hear their conversation clearly as they walked toward it.

"You should have told me right away the Hardy boys were on that plane, instead of waiting until now," Red complained to his cousin.

"How'd I know that Fenton Hardy was investigating you too?" Jivaro asked. "Anyway, didn't your girlfriend just tell you over the phone that their being here has nothing to do with the car operation?"

The two climbed into the sports car.

"Yeah, she did," Red admitted. "When I called to bawl her out for not mentioning they were on the plane, she told me they're in town to check on some missing coin that one of their friends inherited. We'll get the details when we meet her at her apartment."

"Will she be able to get away from the bank?"

"She says she can make it on her lunch hour. The key's under a flowerpot, so we can get in."

Red started the engine, but did not immediately drive off because Jivaro said, "Wait a minute. You think I ought to go with you?"

"Why not?"

"She was on the plane. She's going to recognize me as the hijacker."

"She's not going to squeal on any friend of mine," Red told him. "Don't worry about it." With that, they took off in a cloud of dust.

At the apartment, Joe and Vern had searched everywhere except in the bedroom without finding anything of interest. Now, while going through a dresser drawer, Joe saw a bankbook under a pile of stockings. Opening it, he let out a whistle.

"What's the matter?" Vern asked.

"This is a savings account in Cylvia Nash's name, opened ten years ago. It shows regular deposits of twenty dollars every month, up to last month— except for one!"

Vern shrugged. "So she's a frugal woman. You can't blame her for missing one deposit in ten years."

"I didn't mean she missed one. She made a larger one. On April 12, eight years ago, she put in fifty thousand dollars!"

Vern took the book from his friend's hand to look at it. "Now there's a coincidence! Uncle Gregg put that coin in his safe-deposit box on March 22, just two weeks prior to her big deposit."

Suddenly, they heard a key turn in the front door. Joe hurriedly replaced the bankbook beneath the stockings where he had found it and closed the dresser drawer. Then he and Vern flattened themselves against the wall at either side of the bedroom door.

A male voice that sounded vaguely familiar to Joe said, "We may as well relax. She won't be along for at least fifteen minutes."

Another man grunted an unintelligible reply. The boys were relieved that it wasn't Cylvia who had entered. They would never have been able to pass themselves off as telephone repairmen to her!

Joe signaled to Vern and tiptoed toward the bathroom. When they were both inside, he closed the door as quickly as he could, and went over to the window. He raised it carefully and looked out. They were on the second floor, and the drop to the concrete courtyard was too great to risk.

"Guess we'll have to walk out the front way," the young detective grumbled. "I hope it isn't anybody that knows us. That one voice sounded familiar!"

"Not to me," Vern said. "But do you think we'll get away with it even if they don't know us?"

"Sure. We'll just have to brazen it out," Joe said with determination. "Just say the phone is okay now. If they ask how we got in, we'll tell the truth. The manager let us in."

"Maybe we better wait in here until they leave," Vern suggested.

Joe shook his head. "They're expecting somebody along in fifteen minutes, and it's a woman. Probably Cylvia Nash. If she sees us, it's all over."

Vern nodded. "Okay. Let's try it."

Joe eased open the bathroom door. Deliberately rattling some tools on his belt, he said in a loud voice, "The phone's working all right now. What's our next stop?"

Vern mumbled an address, as they walked into the front room.

"Your phone's—" Joe started to say, but came to an abrupt halt when he saw Red Sluice and Anton Jivaro seated in chairs.

Sluice jumped to his feet instantly. "Those thieves again!" he shouted.

The boys raced for the door, but Sluice got there ahead of them and, with his back firmly planted against it, pulled out a knife!

9 *The Bomb*

Anton Jivaro followed the group. "Thieves?" he said. "What do you mean by that?"

Red pointed his knife at Joe. "That's one of the kids who tried to break into my house last night. Then we caught him in the machine shop at the warehouse this morning. I don't know who the other one is."

"I'll tell you! First of all, they're not thieves!" the hijacker exclaimed. "That's Joe Hardy, and the one with him is named Vern Nelson."

Joe whispered to Vern, "You take the little guy and I'll handle Red."

"You'll handle who?" Red said, raising his knife threateningly.

Suddenly, Anton rushed at Vern and landed three quick blows before the boy could get set. As Vern reeled backward, Joe undid the buckle of his heavily laden tool belt and tossed it at Red. A heavy wrench smashed into the man's toe.

"Ow!" Red yelled, dancing on one foot in pain.

Vern recovered, grabbed Jivaro by both arms and hurled him across the room. The little man crashed into Red and both went down in a tangle.

Joe scooted out the door with Vern right behind him. The boys were running down the stairs four at a time before Red and Anton picked themselves up and took off in hot pursuit.

The elderly woman who managed the apartment house was supervising a gardener weeding the lawn when the boys rushed outside. Both she and the gardener gazed after them in surprise, and almost failed to notice Red Sluice and Anton Jivaro dash out the door. The two hoods stopped suddenly when they saw they would have witnesses. Red hurriedly put away his knife before the manager and the gardener turned around to look at them.

The young detectives jumped into the gray sedan. Joe started the engine, and they took off as fast as they could.

"Sluice and Jivaro are walking to their car real easy," he reported looking back. "Guess they don't want to chance the manager calling the police."

Joe turned a corner before the red sports car started to move. He ducked through an alley, then drove a zigzag course for several blocks. When he was sure he had lost his pursuers, he returned to the hotel.

As they approached their rooms, Joe felt in his coveralls pockets and said, "Uh-oh! Guess what."

"What?"

"My room key was in a section of that tool belt. If they find it, they'll know where we're staying, because the tag on the key shows the hotel."

"I still have my key," Vern said. "I'll let you in my room, and you can go into yours through the connecting door. But we should change hotels once we get Frank and Chet."

After changing back into their regular clothes, the boys drove to the warehouse to relieve their friends. En route they picked up a sack of hamburgers and soft drinks for lunch.

Joe gave a code signal with his horn when they passed the front of the warehouse, then parked down the street. As they walked up the block, Frank emerged from the refrigerator carton and started toward them.

"It's about time," he said as he neared. "Chet's probably half dead of starvation."

Joe grinned. "We've got something to save him," he said, waving the bag of hamburgers. "We'd have been back sooner, if we hadn't run into some problems. Anything happen here?"

"Nothing important. Red Sluice and Anton Jivaro came out and drove off in the sports car. I overheard them talking before they left. They were headed for Cylvia Nash's apartment."

"Wish we'd known that," Joe said ruefully. "We were searching the place when they walked in, and had to fight our way out."

"Searching it? Why?"

"Cylvia's the bank clerk who checked Vern's Uncle Gregg into the vault the day he put the Liberty Head nickel in his safe-deposit box. We found a bankbook in her name showing a fifty-thousand-dollar deposit two weeks later."

"Maybe she stole the coin!" Frank exclaimed.

"Maybe. With the system the bank has, I don't see how she could have, but the timing of that deposit is certainly suspicious."

Together the three walked cautiously around to the alley. Chet was in the shed, looking through the eyehole and playing with his yo-yo absentmindedly. He turned around as they entered.

"Where'd you get the toy?" Joe asked.

"Through a failure in communication. I'd rather

not talk about it." Eyeing the sack Joe was carrying, he sniffed appreciatively. "That smells like hamburgers."

"Five of them," Joe said. "Two for you and one each for the rest of us. Plus four sodas."

As the boys opened the bag to begin eating, Joe asked Chet if he had anything to report. The boy said nothing had happened except that half a dozen workmen had emerged from the warehouse at noon and walked down the alley in the direction of the delicatessen. A half hour later they returned. Chet assumed they had gone for lunch.

After they finished eating, the boys exchanged cameras. Vern was to take over stakeout duty at the rear of the warehouse, while Joe would station himself in the refrigerator carton in front. Chet and Frank decided to return to the hotel.

Leaving Vern in the shed, the Hardys and Chet walked to the car. "Be careful," Joe cautioned. "I left my room key in the tool belt when we were getting away from those hoods, and if they find it, they'll know where we're staying."

As the two drove off, Joe went to the refrigerator carton, settled himself on the wooden box, and put his eye to the view hole.

An hour passed without anyone going in or out of the warehouse. He was getting bored when he heard someone opening the cardboard door behind him.

Jumping to his feet, he whirled with his hands raised in karate stance, then relaxed when he saw it was Vern.

In a low voice Vern said, "Remember that tattooed truck driver your father said was named Crafty Kraft?"

Joe nodded.

"He backed his truck up to the sliding door. I couldn't see what he unloaded, because the hood was right in front of me, but I'll bet it was stolen cars, and I wouldn't be surprised if mine was among them!"

"Maybe we'd better take a look," Joe suggested.

They walked around to the alley. Kraft's truck was still parked there, but the sliding door was closed. After looking both ways to make sure no one was watching, Joe raised the restroom window and peered inside. Seeing it was empty, he climbed in. Vern followed.

Cautiously, Joe peered out into the big, barnlike garage. When he spotted no one nearby, he opened the door far enough for Vern and him to slip through. They crouched behind the same partially dismantled car where the Hardys had concealed themselves earlier.

The office was open and no one was inside.

Glancing around, Joe spotted neither Big Harry nor Crafty Kraft.

Three relatively new cars were parked right next to the back door. Excitedly Vern pointed to a blue sedan. "That's mine!" he whispered.

Suddenly the boys had to crouch low because a workman was headed their way. He went by without seeing them and entered the restroom.

"When he comes out, he'll spot us," Joe pointed out. "We'll have to find another place to hide."

"How about between those cars?" Vern suggested.

Nodding, Joe stood up, glanced toward the crew to make sure no one was looking, and led the way to the newly delivered cars. At that moment, Crafty Kraft and Big Harry rose to their feet right in front of them! They had been in a crouched position, examining the underside of one of the cars. They spotted the boys instantly.

"Hey, you!" Big Harry shouted in a threatening voice, starting toward them.

Joe and Vern bolted for the restroom door, only to find it locked from inside. Before they could run in any other direction, Big Harry grabbed Joe in a bear hug and Crafty Kraft collared Vern. Fighting hard, the boys broke free and began to trade blows with their opponents. Moments later, a number of workmen, alerted by the commotion, converged on them. The young detectives were grabbed and held motionless by a dozen hands.

"Take them into my office," Big Harry ordered.

Frank and Chet, meanwhile, discussed Joe's warning as they rode up in the hotel elevator.

"If they found the key, they could be waiting for us when we walk into our room," Chet said with trepidation. "They could take us off somewhere, and we'd never be seen again."

"You sound like Aunt Gertrude," Frank said. "They wouldn't try to kidnap us here."

"Why not?"

"Because a hotel is too public a place for that kind of thing. How would they get us across the lobby? More likely they'd just bug our rooms so they'd know what our plans are."

"Then we'll look for bugs," Chet concluded with relief.

The boys entered each room cautiously, examining everything with great care. They even checked the heating vents, and unscrewed both the mouthpieces and earpieces of the telephones to make sure no microphones had been planted in them.

"The place is clean," Frank declared finally.

"When do we have to relieve Joe and Vern?" Chet asked.

"We won't. We'll just pick them up about five. I

figure that's when the gang'll close down for the day. If the big boss hasn't appeared by then, he probably won't show up at all. There's no point in staking out the warehouse all night. We'll start again in the morning."

"Suits me," Chet said, flopping down on his bed.

"I'm going to take a shower," Frank announced, and walked through the connecting bathroom into his own room.

His suitcase lay on a small bench against the wall. Deciding to take out some clean clothes before showering, he opened the bag. Instantly there was a puff of smoke, a blinding flash, and a thunderous explosion!

10 Captured

Chet rushed in and saw Frank sitting on the floor with a stunned expression on his face.

"Are you hurt?" the boy asked anxiously.

Frank climbed to his feet. "No, I'm fine." He went over to look into the suitcase. "It was just a scare tactic, I think. All noise and no damage."

Picking up a note that was lying next to the remains of the fake bomb, he read it, then passed it on to Chet. In block letters was printed: GO BACK TO BAYPORT, OR THE NEXT ONE WILL BE REAL!

"They mean business," Chet said nervously.

"So do we," Frank stated in a grim tone. "We won't be going back to Bayport. We'll just make them think we did."

78

"How can we do that?" Chet inquired.

"After we pick up Joe and Vern, we'll check out of here and go to another hotel."

At five o'clock the two friends drove to the warehouse and Frank gave the code honk. Parking down the street, they waited. When Joe and Vern did not appear, Frank walked back to check the refrigerator carton. It was empty, but his camera was lying underneath the wooden crate.

Frank was about to leave when he heard a car drive up. Peering through the view hole, he saw a distinguished-looking man getting out of a Lincoln Continental. Frank took his camera and snapped a picture through the view hole as the man let himself into the warehouse. Then he pocketed the camera.

He returned to their rental car, leaned in the window, and said to Chet, "Joe isn't there, but a guy I'm betting is the kingpin of this operation just went into the place."

"Where do you suppose Joe is?" Chet asked.

"Probably back in the shed with Vern."

Chet got out of the car and they sneaked around to the alley. An eighteen-wheel truck was parked next to the sliding door, but no one was in the shed.

"Maybe they got hungry and went to the deli," Chet suggested.

"We'll check," Frank said with a frown. "But I don't think they'd both take off."

They hurried to the delicatessen, but Joe and Vern were not there. Frank described the two boys to the Chinese proprietor, but the man couldn't remembering seeing anyone who resembled Joe and Vern.

Outside Chet asked, "What do you think?"

"I think they're in trouble, maybe being held prisoner in the warehouse."

"We can't go in there."

"Why not?" Frank asked, heading back up the alley. "Joe and I got in there this morning."

"You got into trouble, too," Chet said. "That place is full of hoods."

Frank stopped next to the warehouse's restroom window. "You stay in the shed, then," he suggested. "I'll go in alone."

The window was already open. Frank made sure the room was empty, then climbed inside. Stealthily, he crept over to the door that opened into the main room.

Hearing a grunting noise behind him, he spun around. Chet was just pulling himself over the sill.

"I thought you didn't want to come," Frank whispered.

"I didn't. But I hate to be alone."

Opening the door a crack, Frank looked into the garage. Workmen were putting down their tools and preparing to go home.

Frank whispered over his shoulder. "They're quitting work. We better move before they start coming in to wash up."

He opened the door far enough to slip through and led the way to the three new cars parked near the back door. The boys crouched out of sight between two of them.

"That's Vern's!" Chet hissed, jerking a thumb at the blue sedan to their left. "It must have been delivered by that truck out there."

"Which means Crafty Kraft's around here somewhere," Frank replied in a low tone.

The boys had left the restroom just in time, since workmen began heading toward it to wash up. Frank and Chet lay low until the last of them had finished and had exited through the front door.

When the big garage was empty, Frank rose to his feet, looked in all directions, and then tiptoed toward the office. Through the open office door, he could see Big Harry behind his desk, talking to two men seated in front of it. One was the tattooed truck driver Fenton Hardy had identified as one of the chief lieutenants of the car-theft ring, Crafty Kraft. The other was the distinguished-looking man who had arrived in the Lincoln Continental.

Frank retreated behind the cars again, where he was out of sight from the office, and motioned Chet to follow him. Quietly, they moved along the rear wall, then made their way around to the office door. They stopped just before they reached it and positioned themselves so that they could hear everything, but not be seen.

A voice that Frank guessed belonged to the distinguished-looking man said, "Who, may I ask, are they?"

"According to their I.D.s, they're Joe Hardy and Vern Nelson," Big Harry replied.

"Joe Hardy! That's one of Fenton Hardy's sons. I thought he was in town on other business."

"So did Red Sluice," Big Harry said. "He told me those kids were here to find some coin that disappeared, but this is the second time we've caught this one prowling around. The first time he was with a different guy, and they both escaped."

"Probably his older brother," a third man said in a raspy voice. Frank assumed this was Crafty Kraft. "I hear they're always together."

"Well, what do you want us to do with these two, sir?" Big Harry asked.

The *sir* told Frank that he had guessed right about the newcomer being the big boss of the car-theft ring.

"They'll have to be kept out of circulation until we finish stripping this shipment," came the reply.

"After that it won't matter, because we can move to another location. But if we turn them loose now, they'll run straight to the police."

"I've got an isolated cottage over on Catalina Island," Big Harry offered.

"That would be excellent. You own a boat, too, don't you?"

"Yes, sir."

"Then run them over there and hold them until further notice. Oh, and while you've got them, you may as well squeeze out any information you can about how much Fenton Hardy has learned about our operation."

"Yes, sir," Big Harry repeated.

There was the sound of a chair scraping. Frank and Chet made a beeline for the nearest hiding place. They hid themselves behind a partially dismantled car and an instant later, the distinguished-looking gentleman stepped from the office.

As he started toward the front door, it opened and Red Sluice came in with Anton Jivaro. The three met halfway across the garage, near enough for Frank and Chet to overhear them.

"Who is this, Red?" the boss asked sharply.

"My old partner, Anton, sir. He started work here today."

Frowning at the little man, the boss said, "You

know my rule about thoroughly checking all prospective employees, Red."

"But he's a very old friend, sir," Red protested. "I can vouch for him."

"I hope so, because we already have a serious security problem. Big Harry and Crafty caught the younger son of Fenton Hardy and a companion inside the warehouse this afternoon."

"Again! Both Hardys were here this morning, but they got away. Who was Joe's companion?"

"Someone named Vern Nelson."

Red and Jivaro looked at each other. "The same pair!" Red said.

"What do you mean?" the boss asked.

"We almost had them earlier today. Did they get away again?"

The boss shook his head. "Not this time. They're trussed up in the machine shop."

"What were they after?"

"I haven't interrogated them, because I prefer not to have my face seen by people outside the organization."

"The older Hardy boy is still around somewhere," Red said, "and so is another friend named Chet Morton."

The boss frowned. "They could be lurking around here. You better search the whole area."

"I think they'd be too scared," Anton Jivaro spoke up. "We left a warning in their hotel room to go back to Bayport."

"Look anyway," the boss instructed.

He continued out the front door while Red and Jivaro went into the office. Frank motioned for Chet to follow him, and the two tiptoed over to the machine shop. They slipped inside and closed the door behind them.

Joe and Vern lay on the floor, tied and gagged!

"I'll take care of them," Frank whispered to Chet. "You'd better open the door just a crack and watch if anyone's coming."

Chet nodded. While Frank removed the gags from the prisoners' mouths, the chubby boy silently turned the doorknob to peek out. Then he gasped.

He was staring directly into Red Sluice's face!

11 Overboard!

Chet tried to close the door, but Red kicked it open with his foot, and the boy jumped back in order to avoid being batted.

Then Red Sluice, Anton Jivaro, Crafty Kraft, and Big Harry poured into the room. Frank had not yet succeeded in loosening either Joe's or Vern's bonds, so it was four against two. There was a fierce struggle but the hoods finally subdued the young detectives, tying their hands behind them.

When the boys were safely bound, Red declared with satisfaction, "You two saved me the trouble of hunting you down."

Crafty Kraft asked, "Now what?"

"Untie the feet of those two so they can walk," Big

Harry ordered, pointing to Joe and Vern. "Then load all four of them on your truck."

"Are we going over to the island now?" Crafty asked.

Big Harry shook his head. "We have to wait until morning because I can't get away tonight. But I want them out of here. They'll be safe tied up on the boat."

Red scowled. "I'd rather get it over with tonight."

"Can you run the boat?" Big Harry countered.

Red shook his head, and then looked hopefully over at his partners. Crafty Kraft and Anton both admitted they knew nothing about boats either.

The boys were put in the rear of the eighteen-wheel truck. Sluice and Jivaro got in with them as guards, while the tattooed Crafty drove.

"Where are we going?" Frank asked Red as the truck began to move.

"Terminal Island," Red told him.

"I thought that was a prison," Joe said.

"There's a federal prison there, but the Los Angeles Harbor's there too."

"What kind of boat does Big Harry have?" Anton Jivaro asked Red.

"A thirty-six-footer with twin diesel engines. Sleeps six and has a cruising range of one thousand miles."

"Will we be going that far?" Chet asked, worried.

"You'll only be going about three miles out," Red told him.

Chet gulped.

"He's only trying to scare you," Frank whispered in the plump boy's ear.

"Speak up if you have anything to say," Red said sharply. Frank fell silent.

They rode for about an hour. When they finally stopped, Crafty Kraft opened the rear door.

"All clear," he announced. "Nobody in sight."

Red and Anton jumped out, and immediately ordered the boys to move. They were parked on a dock containing dozens of boat slips. It was still light enough for them to see that the nearest boat was a large cabin cruiser with *Sea Scorpion* lettered on its bow.

"I have to get the truck off the dock," Crafty Kraft said to Red. "I'll come back with Big Harry in the morning."

He climbed into the vehicle and drove off, while the boys were taken aboard and herded down into the main cabin. Inside there were only two double bunks, but through a hatch they could see that the galley next door contained benches that could be converted into two more bunks.

Red and Anton shoved the boys into the galley

and ordered them to sit down. Then Red pulled out a table that folded into the wall and lowered it between them.

"Chow time," he announced, and began rummaging in the refrigerator. "Nothing but bacon and eggs and bread," he grumbled.

Taking all the ingredients out, Red cooked an unappetizing dinner. He and Anton quickly ate, and then fed the prisoners, whose hands were still tied behind their backs.

After they had eaten, the young detectives were herded back into the main cabin. Red assigned Chet and Vern the two lower bunks, and told Frank and Joe to climb into the upper ones.

"You'll have to untie us before we can make it," Frank objected.

"No way," Red said. "You guys have gotten away from us twice, and I'm not taking any risks. Anton, help me lift them up."

The two men shoved the brothers into the upper bunks and hogtied them securely. In addition, the boys were bound to wall stanchions behind them so that they could not roll from their beds.

When they were finished, Red and Anton went topside, leaving the cabin lights on.

"What do you think they're going to do to us?" Vern asked.

"Take us over to Catalina Island, I guess, where

Big Harry has a secluded cottage," Frank said optimistically. "They're only going to hold us until they finish stripping the cars they have at the warehouse, then they're going to move to another location. As soon as they do that, they figure it will be safe to turn us loose."

"That isn't what Red Sluice said to Chet," Joe stated.

"He was just trying to scare us. We overheard the big boss giving instructions. He wants them to squeeze out of us what Dad has learned about the theft ring so far."

"You saw the big boss?" Joe asked.

"I even took his picture," Frank replied. "I don't know who he is, but he's a kind of rich-looking guy. I just hope those crooks don't take my camera out of my pocket."

Chet said, "I remember him telling Big Harry to get information from Joe and Vern, but he didn't say anything about us."

"We hadn't been captured then, superbrain," Frank told him. "What all of us should keep in mind is that if they make any threats, it's just a bluff to get us to talk. They aren't going to do any more than the big boss ordered them to do."

About nine o'clock, Red and Anton came down again and checked the boys' bonds. Finding them secure, they made up the two bunks in the galley for themselves and turned out the lights. Within minutes both were snoring.

Unable to change position, the four boys slept fitfully. Sometime in the early part of the morning, they heard footsteps on deck. Moments later, Big Harry and Crafty Kraft came below.

Sticking his head into the galley, Big Harry woke his companions.

When Red and Anton were up and dressed, the boys were untied one at a time and told to wash up. Then they were allowed one sweet roll each from a sack Big Harry had brought along.

After their meager breakfast, the young detectives were left sitting in the galley, with only their wrists bound, under the watchful eyes of Red and Anton. Big Harry and Crafty went above and started the engines. About ten minutes after the boys felt the boat pull away from the dock, Crafty called down from above, "The skipper says to bring them topside."

Red and Anton herded the boys on deck. They saw that the boat, with Big Harry at the helm, was headed well out to sea. "Sit with your backs to the rail!" Red ordered. Frank and Chet lowered themselves on the portside, while Joe and Vern leaned against the starboard rail.

Standing over Frank and looking down at him, Crafty Kraft began the interrogation. "How much does your father know about our operation at the warehouse?"

"How could he know anything?" Frank inquired. "He lives in Bayport."

"He sent you and your brother here," the tattooed man said impatiently. "And I'm sure you've phoned him since you found out about us."

"We came here on our own," Joe spoke up. "And we'll give you our word that we haven't talked to him since we arrived."

Crafty turned around to face the boy. "You feel like talking?"

"I have nothing to talk about!"

Crafty told Anton to follow him, and the two went down into the cabin. Shortly they reappeared with two small, rowboat-size anchors.

They dropped them on the deck near the boys' feet. Then, while Anton joined Red and Big Harry at the bridge, Crafty went below again.

When he came back, he was carrying a coil of thin wire in one hand and a pair of wire cutters in the other. Dropping the wire near the anchors, he snipped off four lengths of about four feet each.

"What's that for?" Chet inquired fearfully.

"Nothing, if your friends talk," Crafty told him. "If they don't, we're going to see how well you boys can swim with anchors tied to your bodies."

"Hey, that's murder!" Chet protested.

"So, try calling a cop!" Crafty snarled.

Dropping the wire cutters next to the anchors, the tattooed man went forward to confer with his companions.

The wire cutters were closer to Joe than to any of the others. Glancing toward the bridge, he whispered, "Keep watch and warn me if any of them look this way."

He had just started to inch forward when Frank hissed, "Watch out!"

Joe hurriedly slid back against the rail, just as Crafty Kraft came back to stand over him again.

"Your last chance," he said. "Would you rather talk or go overboard?"

"I have nothing to talk about," Joe said evenly.

The tattooed man kneeled down before the boy and passed a piece of wire around his waist, twisted it tight and fastened an anchor to it. Then he rose to his feet. "I'll let you think about it a while. Soon as we're three miles out, I'll ask you again."

He went to the bridge. As soon as his back was turned, Joe again inched forward on the seat of his pants. Then he swung around and gripped the wire cutters with his right hand. He twisted the jaws of the cutters toward the rope binding his wrists, but found it too awkward in a seated position. Slowly he struggled to his feet.

At that moment, Big Harry spotted a log floating

in the water just ahead and made a sharp turn to port. Frank and Chet both slid toward the starboard rail. Joe started to lose his balance, almost recovered, but then Chet's sliding body crashed into him.

Joe's knees hit the rail and, head first, he pitched overboard!

12 Turned Tables

The younger Hardy took a deep breath just before he hit the water. He sank swiftly, as the weight of the anchor pulled him down. Frantically, he twisted the wire cutters around until the blade gripped the rope binding his wrist. Desperately, he squeezed the handle.

The rope parted, but he was reaching the point where he had to release his breath, and he was still sinking rapidly. Then, as he brought the wire cutters around in front of him, they slipped from his grasp!

In a last-ditch effort, he reached out with his left hand, felt his fingers close over the blades, and guided the tool into his right hand to regrip the handle. Slowly letting out air from his lungs, he shoved the blades of the cutters around the wire and squeezed the handle.

As the anchor dropped away, Joe let go of the wire cutters and thrust himself upward. He had been dragged down so deep that his lungs emptied while he was only halfway to the surface. Rapidly scissoring his legs and using a powerful breast stroke to propel himself upward, he fought the terrible urge to inhale.

He was losing the battle and was on the verge of breathing in water when he suddenly broke the surface. Gasping, he drew in air, released it, and inhaled again. He treaded water as his breathing gradually returned to normal.

The *Sea Scorpion* was a couple of hundred yards away by now, slowly circling, as the men looked for him. He waved one arm and yelled, but it was too far for anyone to see or hear him. He started to swim toward the boat, but it circled farther and farther away. Finally the skipper gave up and continued out to sea.

As the *Sea Scorpion* disappeared from sight, Joe looked around. There was nothing but unending water in all directions. Fortunately the sea was relatively calm, though the water was cold.

Joe guessed that he was three to five miles from shore. If the sea did not get any rougher, he figured he could swim it, providing he stopped for frequent rests and kept in the right direction. He knew the coast was due east, and positioning himself by the sun, he hoped to avoid swimming in circles.

It was still early enough in the morning for the sun to be fairly low. Joe began swimming directly at it.

Meanwhile, aboard the *Sea Scorpion*, there was considerable confusion. Frank, Vern, and Chet anxiously kept shouting out for Joe, horrified at what might happen to him. As Big Harry circled around in search of Joe, he screamed at Crafty Kraft for allowing the accident to happen.

"It was you who made that sudden turn," the tattooed man objected vehemently.

"Why'd you have to tie that anchor to him?" Big Harry yelled.

"I was just trying to scare him."

"We'll see who gets scared when I report this to the boss," Big Harry said grimly. "He didn't want anything like this."

Frank and Chet took advantage of all the confusion and still calling out Joe's name, put their backs together as though to search for him in opposite directions. Determinedly, they began to pull at each other's wrist bindings. But as Big Harry gave up circling and resumed heading out to sea, Red Sluice noticed what was going on.

"Hey, those two are getting loose!" he shouted.

Red ran over to check Chet's bonds, Crafty bent over Frank, and Anton checked Vern. Frank had moved his back against the rail again so that the tattooed man had to approach him from the front. As he leaned forward to swing Frank around by the shoulders, the boy drew his knees to his chest, planted both feet in the man's stomach, and kicked as hard as he could. Crafty was thrown clear across the deck, hit the opposite rail, and did a back flip into the ocean!

"Man overboard!" Red Sluice yelled. "Turn around!"

As the boat began to circle, Anton grabbed a life preserver and tied a line to it. Frank and Chet swung their backs to each other again and Frank frantically picked at the knot binding Chet's wrists. Anton and Red were too busy looking for Crafty over the side to notice.

Frank loosened the knot and the rope fell away. Chet turned around and quickly untied Frank, while Red and Anton still hung over the railing, calling to their partner.

"All right, Harry!" Red shouted. "Slow down!"

Big Harry throttled the engine until the boat was barely moving, and Anton tossed the life preserver overboard. The man in the water grabbed it and Red began to reel in the rope.

Frank whispered to Chet, "Body blocks. Pretend you're on the football field."

Nodding, Chet crouched as though on the scrimmage line. Frank did the same.

"One–two–three, hike!" Frank said.

In unison they drove forward to throw body blocks into the men at the rail. Screaming loudly, both hoods went overboard to join Crafty Kraft in the water.

"Untie Vern," Frank said to Chet in a low voice, and headed for the bridge.

Big Harry, with his back to the action, had not seen his companions go overboard, and the noise of the engine had drowned out the screams and splashes. He seemed to sense, however, that something was wrong, and looked over his shoulder just as Frank came up behind him. Releasing the wheel, he started to spin around, but Frank managed to land a karate chop at the base of his neck.

Without making a sound, Big Harry pitched forward on his face, unconscious. Quickly the boy searched him for weapons. Finding none, Frank took the helm, while Vern and Chet stood at the rail, looking at the hoods in the water.

"Tell them to hold on to the life preserver," Frank called out. "We'll be back for them after we look for Joe."

While the crooks clung to the life ring, Frank steered the *Sea Scorpion* back into the sun, fervently hoping that Joe had been able to free himself with the wire cutters.

A mile to the east Joe had stopped to rest for a time floating on his back.

Out of the corner of his eye he caught sight of something sliding past him in the water, but did not get a good enough look to identify what it was. Letting his feet down until he was treading water, he turned in the direction the thing had moved, but saw nothing marring the gently rolling surface of the water. He decided it must have been his imagination and started to swim toward the sun again.

Then a movement to his left brought him to a halt. Treading water, he looked that way. A large gray fin broke the surface and swam widely around him.

With his heart pounding, Joe watched the fin going around again, this time in a narrower circle. The shark had spotted him when it originally went by, and was now closing in.

He submerged in order to get an underwater look at the beast. An enormous man-eating white shark over twenty feet long passed him no more than a dozen feet away.

Surfacing, Joe watched as the great fin cut the

water in a wide arc that took it fifty yards beyond him, then swung back in his direction. This time it moved in a straight line, directly toward him!

As the fin neared, he dived in a desperate attempt to swim beneath it. But the shark had a fix on him now. It dived too, opening its enormous jaws wide!

13 Dolphin Rescue

Joe froze in terror. The shark was almost upon him, when he suddenly saw a dark shape on his right, streaking in like a torpedo. Thinking it was another shark, Joe gave up all hope. But the shape, instead of attacking him, struck the shark's midsection. The monster veered aside, and even underwater Joe could hear a loud click as the enormous jaws snapped shut only inches away from him.

The dark shape moved away as fast as it had come in, only to be replaced by another torpedo-like object. It too drove into the shark's side at breakneck speed, then scooted off again. In rapid order, four more speeding forms bludgeoned the man-eater's side, making it flounder almost onto its back before it fled in panic.

Joe surfaced to see the gray fin moving away at express-train speed. It kept going until it disappeared from sight.

Then a graceful, hard-snouted figure arched through the air ten feet over Joe's head and came down in such a perfect dive that it hardly made a splash. Five similar shapes performed the same acrobatics, their crescent-shaped mouths seeming to grin down at Joe as they soared above him.

It was a school of six dolphins, the mortal enemies of sharks, but friends to humans. Joe remembered reading how dolphins occasionally attacked sharks by butting them at high speed with their hard snouts, sometimes even killing them by rupturing their hearts.

The dolphins continued to cavort about him, playfully showing off their acrobatic skill. Joe raised his hands above water to applaud loudly.

Meanwhile, Frank had headed the *Sea Scorpion* into the sun.

"You don't think Joe could have drowned, do you?" Chet asked, shivering at the thought.

"He had the wire cutters in his hand when he went overboard," Frank said, his face drawn and his eyes clouded with fear. "If he acted fast, he could have cut both the rope and the wire around his waist in time. We can only hope."

Chet glanced around. The lump in his stomach

began to ache violently and his voice trembled. "Even i-if he got free of that anchor, how would we find him way out here? We could pass fifty yards from him without spotting him."

"We'll start circling when we get back to where he was knocked overboard."

"If you can figure out where that is. I couldn't."

"I don't think we sailed more than a mile beyond him," Frank said. "I admit our starting point will be a blind guess, but we'll circle from there in wider and wider loops. We ought to hit the right spot eventually."

"Suppose we don't?"

"We'll run in and call the Coast Guard. They'll send up helicopters to scour the whole area. From the air, he'll be a lot easier to see."

When they came to the spot where Frank figured Joe had been thrown overboard, he throttled down until the boat was barely moving.

"Okay," he said to Chet. "You and Vern take posts on opposite sides of the boat and start looking."

Chet moved back amidship to relay this instruction to Vern. Chet took the starboard side and Vern the port side as Frank steered the boat in ever-widening circles. Both boys strained their eyes intently looking out over the water.

When the circle had reached a half mile in diameter with no sign of Joe, Frank became discouraged. "I guess we better leave it up to the Coast Guard," he said, his face ashen white.

"Wait. There's something over there!" Vern suddenly called out.

He pointed into the distance, and at once Frank reversed engines to bring the boat to a halt.

"It's not Joe," Chet said glumly. "It's something jumping in and out of the water. In fact a lot of somethings."

Frank squinted his eyes, and peered under his hand to see what Chet was talking about.

"Sea lions?" he asked.

"Why don't we go see?" Vern suggested.

Advancing the throttle, Frank steered the boat in the direction of the jumping animals.

As they neared, Chet said, "It's a school of porpoises."

"Dolphins, I think," Frank said.

"What's the difference?"

"Dolphins are porpoises, but porpoises aren't necessarily dolphins," Frank explained. "It's like a nickel is a coin, but a coin isn't necessarily a nickel."

Vern said, "He means dolphins are a special kind of porpoise."

By now, they were within fifty yards of the cavorting dolphins. Chet exclaimed, "Hey, there's something in the water they're jumping over!"

Frank pulled the boat in closer.

"Hey, look! It's Joe!" Chet yelled to the others.

Either the approach of the boat, or the boys' relieved shouts, frightened the dolphins away. They raced off in formation, arcing in and out of the water as though they were riding some invisible roller coaster.

Frank slowed the *Sea Scorpion*, reversed engines, and came to a stop within a few feet of his brother. Joe swam over and was pulled aboard by Chet and Vern.

"We thought you were a goner," Chet said happily, pounding his friend on the back.

"I will be, if you keep that up," an exhausted Joe told him, moving out of range.

"Too bad we scared off your friends," Vern said. "It looked like you were all having a good time."

"They saved my life by running off a shark," Joe declared. "How'd you manage to turn the tables?"

"Brains, pure brains," Chet said, tapping his forehead.

"Yeah, but not yours," Vern said. "It was Frank's." He told Joe what had happened.

Frank headed the boat back to the spot where they had left their attackers, while Joe went below in search of dry clothing. He did not find any, but discovered a pair of sneakers that fit him. He would just have to put up with being wet until he got back to the hotel.

Soon the *Sea Scorpion* pulled up near the trio in the water.

"Like to come back aboard?" Chet invited.

"Please," Red Sluice said in a frightened voice. "I can't swim."

"Want us to throw you one of these anchors?" Chet asked.

"Cut the comedy, Chet," Frank called over his shoulder. "Bring them aboard one at a time, and tie each one up before you pull out the next."

"Roger," Chet said. "Come on, Red."

"But first bring out that knife you carry and hold it up," Vern added.

Red let loose of the life ring with one hand to get his knife.

"Drop it," Vern ordered.

Red released his grip and the knife sank into the water.

"You have any weapons, Maharaja?" Chet asked.

"No," the little man said.

"How about you, Crafty?"

The tattooed man shook his head.

"We'll check both of you when you come aboard," Chet warned. "If either of you have anything, we'll toss you back in the water."

"We're not carrying anything," Crafty insisted.

"Okay," Chet called to Frank.

Frank maneuvered the boat right next to the trio.

Chet leaned over to offer Red Sluice a hand. As he pulled him aboard, he twisted the man's right arm behind his back. Vern took hold of the left one and they forced Red face down. After binding his wrists with one of the pieces of rope that had been used on them, they searched his pockets but found no gun or other knives.

"You're next, Crafty," Chet said, leaning over the rail to offer the tattooed man a helping hand.

When Crafty was aboard, they bound his hands and searched him in the same manner. He was carrying no weapons, either.

Finally, they pulled up Anton and gave him the same treatment. Then Chet reached down to retrieve the life preserver and dropped it on the deck.

After arranging the three with their backs to the rail, far enough apart so that they could not untie each other, Chet and Vern went forward to Big Harry, who was still unconscious. He began to wake up just as they finished binding his wrists behind him. Then Frank headed the boat in.

It was close to noon when he berthed the *Sea Scorpion*. After it was tied up, the boys walked a few yards along the dock beyond earshot of the four captives in order to discuss what to do with them. Chet was for turning them over to the authorities immediately.

"We decided not to call in the police until we knew who the big boss of the car theft ring is," Joe reminded him.

"Chet and I did find out," Frank said.

"You only saw him," Joe insisted. "You don't know who he is."

"I snapped his picture from inside that refrigerator carton. I had been looking for you when he drove up in a big car and went into the warehouse."

"How do you know it was the big boss?" Vern asked.

"We sneaked into the warehouse and overheard him talking to Big Harry and Crafty Kraft. That's how we learned you guys were tied up in the machine shop."

"But you don't know his name," Joe said.

"That doesn't matter," Frank told him. "When I get the film developed, I'll turn it over to the police. They should be able to find out who he is. In the meantime, we can't keep those four guys tied up, and we can't let them loose, either. Seems to me we have to turn them in."

"I guess so," Joe agreed. "Wonder if there's a phone around here."

Vern pointed to a large building at the edge of the dock area, about fifty yards away. "Maybe there."

"You guys go check," Frank suggested. "I'll stand guard over our prisoners."

Joe, Chet, and Vern headed for the large building. As they neared, they saw that it was a boat tackle shop. Chet stuck his head in the door and asked a clerk if he had a public phone.

"Out back," the clerk told him.

The three went around the building and found a phone booth. Joe took a dime out of one of his wet pockets, dialed the operator, and asked for the police.

At the dock, Frank stood alongside the boat, occasionally glancing at the prisoners to make sure they were in the same positions. After a time, he decided to go back aboard.

As soon as he stepped on the deck, he realized they had not searched the prisoners as thoroughly as they should have. Crafty Kraft's right pant leg was pushed up above his knee to disclose a leather sheath strapped to his calf. The sheath was empty and he held an eight-inch hunting knife in his hand!

He had already cut the prisoners' bonds, and now all four jumped to their feet and rushed at Frank!

Big Harry and Red Sluice were in the lead. Frank ducked under a looping right thrown by Big Harry, grabbed the man's wrist, and flipped him over his shoulder onto the deck. Whirling to face Red, he fended a blow and shoved him into Crafty and Anton, who were right behind the redheaded man.

While the three were untangling themselves,

Frank thought quickly. He knew there was no way he could win against these four opponents. Just as he saw Big Harry painfully climb to his feet, he took a running jump onto the dock and, picking himself up, raced away.

Big Harry chased after the boy, and the other three hoods followed in hot pursuit.

But Frank had a good lead. When he was halfway between the boat and the tackle shop, Joe, Chet, and Vern came around the corner. Immediately seeing Frank's predicament, they ran up as fast as they could.

The hoods were too tired to stomach another fight, though, and turning, they rushed back toward the boat.

By the time Chet, Vern, and Joe reached Frank, Big Harry was jumping aboard. Seconds later, he started the engine, while his partners were hastily casting off lines.

"Come on!" Frank shouted. "Don't let them get away!"

The four boys raced for the boat. But Red, Anton, and Crafty hopped aboard just before the boys got there, and the *Sea Scorpion* backed from the slip.

The foursome halted at the edge of the dock and watched in frustration as Big Harry swung the boat around and opened the throttle wide!

14 A Magical Disappearance

As the boat disappeared from sight, Joe asked, "How'd they get loose?"

"We didn't search them well enough," Frank said. "Crafty had a knife strapped to his leg."

"Well, at least that settles the argument about whether or not to turn them over to the police," Chet said philosophically.

"Did you call them?" Frank asked Joe.

His younger brother nodded. "They said they'd be right over."

The boys walked back to the boat tackle shop to await the arrival of the police. A paddy wagon and a squad car showed up a few minutes later. Two uniformed officers got out of the car, one middle-aged and wearing sergeant's stripes, the other a young rookie.

"Which one of you phoned in?" the sergeant asked.

"I did," Joe said.

"Your name's Joe Hardy?"

"Yes, sir," Joe said and introduced the other boys.

"I'm Sergeant Kelly and my partner's Jim Olsen." The officer looked from Joe to Frank. "Are you the famous detectives?" he asked.

"Our father's Fenton Hardy," Frank admitted.

"I've heard a lot about him, and you two also. Where are these kidnappers?"

"They got away," Frank confessed. "It was my fault because I was guarding them. One of them had a knife strapped to his leg that we didn't find when we searched him. He cut himself and the others loose and they sailed off in the boat."

"Maybe you'd better tell us the whole story," Sergeant Kelly suggested. He turned to his companion. "Looks like we won't need the paddy wagon, Olsen. Tell Ralph he can take off."

"Sure, Sarge." The young policeman went over to deliver the message to the driver, who left immediately. Running back to the group, he listened to their story.

The boys told everything that had happened, going back to the theft of Vern's car in Bayport.

When they finished, Sergeant Kelly said, "This is a matter for the auto-theft division. But first, I want you to describe the kidnappers and their boat so the Coast Guard can begin a search."

The boys related every detail they could remember, and the sergeant radioed their report to headquarters.

When he hung up the radio mike, he said, "Now we'll take you to Parker Center to talk to someone in the auto-theft division. Okay?"

"Can we stop at our hotel on the way?" Joe asked. "I'm soaking wet."

The sergeant grinned. "You do look like a drowned rat. Sure, we'll give you time to clean up."

The young detectives crowded into the back seat of the squad car and were driven to their hotel. Since they had slept in their clothes, they all decided to change. Sergeant Kelly told them to take their time.

"There's no rush," he said. "The whole police force plus the Coast Guard are looking for the kidnappers, and that warehouse you told us about won't go away."

"Then we have time for lunch," Chet said, his eyes lighting up. "It's almost two P.M."

"Good idea," Jim Olsen said. "We haven't eaten either."

Chet gave him a delighted look, and Vern

114

laughed. "You just made a lifelong friend, Officer Olsen."

To save time they ordered from room service. The boys had all finished cleaning up and dressing when the food arrived.

After lunch, they were driven to Parker Center, the police administration building. The officers took them to the auto-theft division squad room on the third floor and left them with a tall and somewhat stiff detective named Lieutenant Harold Frisby.

When they repeated their story, he asked them to describe the exact location of the warehouse. Then he picked up his desk phone and asked the switchboard operator to get him the district attorney.

"Hi, Jud," he said into the phone. "I finally have a lead on that nationwide car-theft ring we've been after for so long. I need a search warrant." He gave the address of the warehouse.

As soon as he hung up, he called the Metro division, asking for a squad of a dozen uniformed policemen to accompany him on a raid. "I won't need them for about an hour, because I'm waiting for the district attorney's office to send over a warrant," he added.

When he hung up the second time, Frank asked, "Can we go on the raid?"

The detective shook his head. "No civilians

allowed. There may be shooting. I'll have you dropped back at your hotel."

"Our car's parked near the warehouse," Frank said. "We'd rather be dropped there."

"All right," Lieutenant Frisby agreed.

"As long as we're right there, can we watch the raid from outside?"

The detective gave him an amused look. "You're determined to get in on it one way or another, I see. All right, you can watch from across the street. But you're not going to talk me into letting you participate in the raid."

When the search warrant arrived, Lieutenant Frisby and the four boys took the elevator to the basement garage, where they found three carloads of uniformed policemen with riot guns. The boys got into a fourth car with Lieutenant Frisby, and he led the way to the warehouse at the edge of Old Chinatown.

When they reached the street fronting the warehouse, Frank pointed to the building and said, "That's it." Then he indicated the gray sedan a block beyond the warehouse. "And that's our car."

Lieutenant Frisby parked behind the sedan and the three squad cars pulled up next to him. Everyone got out, and the lieutenant addressed the uniformed sergeant in charge of the riot squad.

116

"Post five men in the back and five in front," he ordered. "Then you and I'll go in."

"Yes, sir," the sergeant said.

Picking five officers, he told them to walk around to the alley and cover the rear of the building. After another five were selected to cover the front, only one was left. The sergeant designated him to accompany him and the lieutenant inside.

Lieutenant Frisby gave the men time to get into position. While waiting, he told the boys to move in back of the parked police cars in case there was any shooting. The young detectives crouched behind the two nearest to the warehouse.

The lieutenant checked his watch. "Okay, let's go now," he said to the two officers. Quickly, the lieutenant and his companions crossed the street.

He tried the front door and looked surprised when he found it unlocked. Opening it, he drew his gun and stepped inside. The two men followed.

Ten minutes passed with no sound from the warehouse. The boys heard one of the men ask uneasily, "Think we should bust in there?"

"The lieutenant said to wait," another one answered.

Then Lieutenant Frisby and his two companions reappeared. He no longer had his gun in his hand, and the two men carried their riot guns pointed

117

downward. They recrossed the street, slowly.

"False alarm, fellows," the sergeant said. "Head back to Parker Center."

Apparently, he had already told the men out back that the raid was called off, because they came around from the alley and climbed into the squad cars. The young detectives watched open-mouthed as all three cars drove off.

"I don't get it," Joe said to the lieutenant.

"Follow me," the detective said peremptorily.

He led them across the street, opened the warehouse's front door, and they all went in. The boys gaped in astonishment. The big, barnlike main room was completely empty!

The lieutenant crossed to the door to their left and opened it.

"This the machine shop you mentioned?" he asked.

Crowding around the door, the boys stared in at the empty room.

"It was," Frank said, a sinking feeling in his stomach.

The lieutenant led them to the office. A skinny old man smoking a corncob pipe sat in Big Harry's chair with his feet up on the desk.

"Back again, Lieutenant?" he said with a grin.

"This is Mr. Jonas Moapes," Lieutenant Frisby said. "Mr. Moapes, would you mind repeating to these four what you told me your job was here?"

"Sure," the old man said agreeably. "I'm the caretaker."

"And how long have you held that job?"

"Three months, ever since the last people who rented the place went out of business."

"What's been in here since?"

"Nothing," the old man said. "The place has been empty."

"That's a lie!" Chet blurted out. The caretaker merely shrugged.

15 Spare Parts For Sale

All four boys were in a state of shock as they left the warehouse with Lieutenant Frisby. Outside he halted and, looking from Frank to Joe, said, "If you two weren't the sons of such a famous father, I would arrest you for filing a false report."

"But the crooks *were* using this warehouse," Joe protested. "Somehow they must have known we were coming."

"We didn't just dream this, Lieutenant," Vern spoke up. "How do you explain our being kidnapped and being taken aboard that boat?"

"I think you dreamed that too," the lieutenant said shortly, and strode toward his car.

After watching him drive away, the boys disconsolately walked up the street to their own automobile. There was dead silence as they returned to the hotel. Upstairs they gathered in the Hardys' room.

"Maybe we did dream the whole thing," Chet suggested.

"Don't be silly," Frank said. "That old man is in with the crooks. They knew the jig was up when we got away, unless they discredited us with the police. And they were clever enough to do it. While Lieutenant Frisby waited for that warrant, they cleared the place out and installed the fake caretaker."

"Let's go back and question Mr. Moapes," Joe said. "Maybe we can shake his story."

"First, let's change hotels," Chet said. "After our encounter with those crooks, I don't feel safe here anymore."

All agreed that this was a good idea. Checking out, they drove to another hotel a few blocks away and again moved into connecting rooms.

When they were settled, Joe suggested that they phone home to report the change, so that their father would know how to get in touch with them if necessary. Frank made the call and his mother answered. She said Fenton Hardy was still on his secret mission, but that she was expecting a call at any time, and would relay this new number to him.

Driving back to the warehouse, the boys parked

121

and tried the front door. It was locked, so they drove around to the alley. They found the back door locked too.

Joe tried the restroom window, which was open. "I wonder why they don't ever lock this too. We've used it twice already," he commented as he climbed over the sill, followed by Chet and Vern.

Frank went in last. Examining the window, he answered Joe's question. "The latch part of the lock is missing!"

The elderly Jonas Moapes was no longer in the building.

"I knew he was a plant," Frank said. "They stuck him in here just long enough to con the police into believing we were crazy."

The boys examined the building thoroughly, ending up in the office where Joe began opening desk drawers. All were empty except the top center one, and the only thing it had in it was an empty matchbook cover. Joe shut the drawer and tossed the matchbook cover on the desk.

Frank picked it up to look at it. On the front was an advertisement for the Admax Wholesale Auto Parts Company of Studio City.

"Hey, look at this," he said, handing it back to Joe.

After reading the ad, Joe said, "It could be a lead.

Maybe it's the outlet for their stolen spare parts!"

Chet and Vern examined Joe's find, too. "It must be," Chet said with enthusiasm. "They have to have some place to get rid of the stuff they steal."

"Let's visit the Admax Wholesale Auto Parts Company," Frank suggested.

The store was on a quiet street off Ventura Boulevard, near Laurel Canyon. It was a long, one-story building with ADMAX WHOLESALE AUTO PARTS painted on a plate glass window.

Parking across the street, Joe told the others to wait while he scouted around. He went to peer in the window, then immediately returned.

He said, "It's the gang's outlet, all right."

"How do you know?" Frank asked.

"Red Sluice is behind the counter!"

At that moment, a chauffeured limousine drove up before the store and a bent old man in expensive clothing got out and went inside.

"Let's sneak around back and see what we can find out," Frank said to Joe.

"Here we go again," Chet said. "I suppose you want me behind the wheel in case we have to take off fast."

"You got it," Frank said with a grin.

There was an alley running alongside the building. Frank and Joe walked to the rear and saw a truck entrance with a sliding door, similar to the one in the back of the Old Chinatown warehouse. It was partially open.

The boys peeked into a large room running the full width of the building. Obviously it was the storeroom, because it was full of auto parts, including complete engines. Parked against the right wall were the three almost new cars, including Vern's blue sedan, that had originally been unloaded at the warehouse.

Crafty Kraft and Anton Jivaro were placing small parts on shelves along the left wall, and the elderly Jonas Moapes was sweeping with a push broom, his back turned toward the boys. He finished just as they looked in, and disappeared through a door that presumably led to the store in front.

Seeing no one else, the boys quietly moved inside and bent down low as they crept along an aisle formed between a row of car engines and stacks of radiators.

In addition to the door straight ahead, which led into the store, there was a second door off to their right. It stood wide open, and through it they noticed the elegantly dressed, bent old man who had arrived in the chauffeured limousine. He was seated before a desk with his back to the door, facing someone the boys could not see.

They moved up alongside the door to listen, hidden from view by a stack of radiators.

The old man said in a creaky voice, "The Merriweather Auto Repair Shop chain is almost nationwide, Mr. Knotts. Surely you've heard of us."

"Sorry, Mr. Merriweather," Big Harry replied in an apologetic tone. "I don't recall seeing your ads."

"Probably because California is one of the four states where we have no shops. We plan to correct that by opening a dozen next month. That is going to require a tremendous supply of parts."

"I'm sure we can serve you satisfactorily," Big Harry said, his tone suddenly becoming ingratiating.

"I didn't make my fortune by beating around the bush," the old man creaked. "So I'll get right to the point. The Merriweather shops are able to undercut all competition because we buy our spare parts cheaper. I ask no questions about where they come from, and I don't care if they're new, so long as they look new. Do you follow me?"

"I think so," Big Harry said cautiously.

"But I pay only half the regular wholesale price."

"We're a discount house, Mr. Merriweather. I'm sure we can make a deal."

"My main need in the beginning is reconditioned

engines that will pass for new," the old man said. "Got any in stock?"

"I'll show you," Big Harry offered.

There was the sound of chairs scraping back. Hurriedly the boys ducked. Big Harry and the old man emerged from the office and slowly moved along the aisle, their backs to the two boys.

Big Harry said, "As you can see, we have a large selection. And the way we clean them up, I doubt that even an expert mechanic could tell they're not brand new."

Taking out a small notebook, the old man peered at an engine and wrote something down. Slowly moving along the line, he continued to make notes.

Finally putting away the notebook, he said, "I guess that's enough of a list for now. I'll go over it with my chief parts buyer, and let you know tomorrow how many and what type engines we'll need."

Suddenly, the boys were grabbed from behind. With a gasp, they tried to turn and face their attackers, but they were held so tightly that moving was impossible!

16 Outwitted

Looking over his shoulder, Frank saw that it was the powerfully built Crafty Kraft who held him in a bear hug. Again he struggled, but was unable to break loose.

Anton Jivaro had a half nelson on Joe, but the little man was no match for his larger opponent. Raising his right foot, Joe slammed his heel into the man's knee. With a howl of pain, Anton broke his grip and backed away.

Hearing the commotion, Big Harry and his aged customer both turned around. As Joe started to go to Frank's aid, Big Harry rushed at him.

Suddenly, the old man clutched his chest. "My heart!" he cried, falling down.

He collapsed in a way similar to an illegal football clip, against the back of Big Harry's legs. The big man lost his balance and landed flat on his face.

Joe got a headlock on Crafty Kraft from behind and pulled him away from Frank. As he released the headlock, he punched the tattooed man in the back, causing him to trip over Big Harry.

Then the boys ran for the door, dashed out, and hurried along the alley to the front. They were across the street and in the car by the time Big Harry and Crafty Kraft burst into sight.

Chet had started the engine when he saw his friends coming, and pulled away before the pursuers could cross the street.

"Good work, Chet," Frank said.

"Head for Parker Center."

Chet turned up Laurel Canyon Boulevard toward the Ventura Freeway. "What happened?" he asked.

"We got caught poking around. All four kidnappers are there. Vern's car is too. Even old Mr. Moapes is there. I have no doubt that the Admax Company is the outlet for what the crooks steal."

Joe added, "Incidentally, we learned Big Harry's last name. It's Knotts."

At Parker Center they found Lieutenant Frisby in the auto-theft division squad room. Frowning at the boys, he said, "You four again?"

"We solved the mystery of the empty warehouse,"

Frank said, handing him the matchbook cover. "They moved everything to this place."

After examining the advertisement, the lieutenant shook his head. "How does this fit in with the warehouse being empty for the last three months?"

"The old man lied," Joe said. "He's the janitor at Admax. The crooks stuck him in the warehouse just to discredit us."

Frank added, "Not only that, but all the men who kidnapped us are at this very minute working at Admax."

"Maybe you better tell me the whole story," Lieutenant Frisby suggested.

When Frank and Joe finished, he looked less doubtful but was not yet completely convinced.

"I'm not going to go off half-cocked by setting up another raid," he told them. "But I'm willing to check it out. You boys can lead me there in your car."

They took the elevator to the basement garage, and the lieutenant drove them around to where they had left their car on the visitors' parking lot. From there he followed them to Studio City.

The five entered the wholesale parts store together. A plump man the boys had never seen before was behind the counter. Lieutenant Frisby showed him his I.D.

"Your manager in?" he asked.

"Just a moment," the plump man said, and disappeared into the back.

"Is he one of your kidnappers?" the lieutenant asked when the clerk was out of sight.

The boys shook their heads. "He wasn't here before," Joe said. "Red Sluice was waiting on customers."

The clerk came back with a tall, gangling man. Offering a handshake to the lieutenant, he said, "I'm Osgood Admax, Lieutenant, the store's owner. What's the problem?"

Lieutenant Frisby turned to the boys. "Is he one of them?"

They shook their heads again.

"Mr. Admax," the officer asked, "you employ a janitor named Jonas Moapes?"

In a puzzled voice the man said, "I don't even know anyone by that name. Except for a part-time bookkeeper, my only employee is Melvin here." He nodded toward the plump clerk. "What's this all about?"

Indicating the boys, the detective said, "These young men have made some serious charges against you. They claim this place is an outlet for auto parts stripped from stolen cars."

"That's a lie!" Admax objected indignantly.

"Mind if we take a look at your storeroom?" Lieutenant Frisby asked. "Or do I need a warrant?"

"I don't mind at all. We have nothing to hide."

Raising a hinged section of the counter to let the officer and the boys through, Admax led them into the back room. Frank and Joe gazed around in consternation. The three stolen cars were gone, and all the engines had disappeared. Everything else that had been there previously, however, still seemed to be in place.

"They've moved out the hottest stuff!" Joe exclaimed. "They knew we'd go to the police, so they got rid of it fast."

"What are you talking about, young man?" Osgood Admax inquired.

Pointing to the side wall, Joe said, "An hour ago three stolen cars were parked there."

"And over a dozen engines were lined up here," Frank added. He pointed to the spot. "You got them out of here because you knew the serial numbers would prove they were stolen!"

Drawing himself up with dignity, the store owner said, "I have invoices for every item in this place. Lieutenant, you are free to examine my records."

"They won't show anything," Joe said angrily. "Invoices are easy to forge. They got everything out of here that had serial numbers on it, so there's no way to prove the rest of this stuff is hot."

The lieutenant's voice was just as angry when he

said, "What kind of game are you boys playing?" He turned to the gangling man. "Accept my apologies, Mr. Admax."

"Of course," the man said graciously. "You were only doing your duty." He frowned at the young detectives. "I don't know why you are trying to cause me trouble, but if you try it again, I'll sue you for defaming my character."

"Let's get out of here," Joe muttered in disgust. "I don't think he has any character."

Outside Lieutenant Frisby said in a grim tone, "Now I want you four to come with me."

As they followed the detective's car, Chet asked worriedly from the back seat, "Think he's running us in for filing a false report?"

"How could he?" Frank said. "We haven't filed any."

"He seems to think we have," Chet said.

But the lieutenant was not leading them back to Parker Center. Instead he drove to the warehouse on the edge of Old Chinatown. He parked in front and Frank pulled in behind him.

When they got out of the car, Frank said, "I've got a feeling we're in for another surprise."

The lieutenant tried the front door and found it unlocked. As they went inside, Joe said to Frank, "I have a feeling your feeling is right."

They headed for the office. The elderly Jonas Moapes was seated behind the desk with his feet up, again smoking his corncob pipe.

"Why, hello, Lieutenant!" he exclaimed cordially. "What is it this time?"

"Nothing," the officer said, and, turning abruptly, he stalked out of the place.

The lieutenant climbed into his car and drove off. The four boys looked at each other.

"Now what?" Chet asked.

"Now that he's discredited us again," Frank said, "that old man won't stick around here long. Let's tail him wherever he goes."

Since they did not know whether Jonas Moapes would come out the front or the back door, Frank drove the car to the side street and parked so that they could see up the alley. Then Joe posted himself at the corner, where he could observe the front and signal to the others if the old man should appear.

About fifteen minutes later, Frank lightly beeped the horn. Joe hurried to the car and climbed in next to him. Looking up the alley, he saw Crafty Kraft's eighteen-wheeler backing up to the sliding door.

As they watched, the tattooed man lowered the ramp, and three coveralled workmen emerged. Using a dolly, they began unloading car engines and wheeling them into the warehouse.

When they were finished, Crafty pulled the truck

out of the way, but left it in the alley. The vehicle had blocked the boys' view of what was beyond it, but now they saw that the three stolen cars were parked there, waiting for the truck to move. They were driven into the warehouse by Sluice, Jivaro, and Big Harry Knotts.

Joe got out of the car.

"Where're you going?" Frank asked.

Pointing to the delicatessen right across the street, at the edge of the alley, Joe said, "To call Lieutenant Frisby."

There was a pay phone on the wall of the small shop. Dropping in a dime, Joe dialed Parker Center and asked for the auto-theft division.

A voice answered, "Lieutenant Frisby."

"This is Joe Hardy," the young detective said. "We're still at the warehouse. Those stolen car engines were just unloaded from a truck, and the three cars were driven in there a few minutes ago. The crooks must figure that since you've already checked the warehouse twice, you won't check it again."

"They're right about that," the detective said and hung up.

Joe walked back to the car, discouraged and frustrated. As he climbed in, Crafty Kraft started the truck. It was facing their way, and while it was too far for the driver to notice the four boys, he would be able to see them once he got to the mouth of the alley. Frank hurriedly pulled away.

"We'll circle the block and come in behind them," he said. "What did the lieutenant say, Joe?"

"He didn't believe me," Joe said glumly. "Who's in the truck?"

"Everybody, including old Mr. Moapes. They locked up the building."

Vern said, "If Lieutenant Frisby isn't going to do anything, what's the point of following the truck? He won't react when we tell him where it went, either."

"I guess you're right," Frank agreed. "We may as well go back to the hotel. It's getting late anyway."

Some time later, they all gathered in the Hardys' room to discuss their next step.

"Let's wait until we hear from our dad," Frank suggested. "We'll give him all the information and let him contact Lieutenant Frisby. Hopefully, the lieutenant will believe *him*."

There was a knock on the door. Joe went to open it, and gaped in surprise.

Standing in the hall was the well-dressed, bent old man, Mr. Merriweather!

17 The Old Man

Without a word, the old man moved into the room. Joe regained his composure. "I thought you'd be in the hospital, Mr. Merriweather," he said.

Merriweather shut the door behind him and said in his creaky voice, "I had a miraculous recovery from my heart attack."

Then he laughed and straightened up. He pulled off his white wig and false white eyebrows, and used a handkerchief to wipe away the makeup that made him look wrinkled.

"Dad!" Frank and Joe cried out. "How did you find us?"

"I went to your previous hotel," the private

detective said. "When I found you'd checked out, I phoned home."

"B-but what were you doing at Admax, Mr. Hardy?" Chet asked.

"Getting evidence against the car-theft gang! When you saw me writing in my notebook, I was taking down the serial numbers of engines. I just phoned the Division of Motor Vehicles in New York State, and all of them are from stolen cars. What were *you* doing there?"

The boys related the results of their investigation, and how the crooks had managed to trick the police into thinking they were lying.

"If only Lieutenant Frisby had gotten to the warehouse about fifteen minutes later this afternoon," Chet said. "He would have caught them moving the stolen goods back in."

"I doubt it," Mr. Hardy disagreed. "The timing was deliberate on the part of the crooks. Probably they were waiting somewhere with that truck and the three stolen cars for an all-clear phone call from the phony caretaker."

"And now Lieutenant Frisby won't even talk to us anymore," Joe complained.

"I think he'll listen to me," Mr. Hardy said.

Dialing Parker Center, he asked for the officer, holding the phone so that the boys could listen in.

137

When he got Lieutenant Frisby on the line, he explained who he was.

"Oh, yes," the lieutenant said. "I've heard a lot about you, sir. But I'm afraid I've been having some trouble with your sons and a couple of their friends."

"I know, Lieutenant. I'm calling from their hotel room. The gang has been cleverly fooling you. Everything the boys told you was true."

"But the evidence against their story was overwhelming," the detective protested.

"Nevertheless, it was false evidence. As the boys told you, those stolen cars and things *were* at Admax. I not only saw them, but by pretending to be a crooked buyer, I got the serial numbers of the engines. I just checked with the New York State DMV, and all are listed as stolen. Right now, the three cars that have not been stripped yet and the engines are at the warehouse in Old Chinatown."

"Your word is good enough for me," the lieutenant said. "My search warrant for that place is still good, so I won't have to wait for a new one. Can you meet me there right away?"

"I'll be glad to."

Mr. Hardy, who had turned in his rented limousine, had come in a taxi, so they drove to the warehouse in the boys' car. Lieutenant Frisby was already there with a half dozen policemen.

After shaking hands with Fenton Hardy, the lieutenant said, "The rear doors are locked. I guess we'll have to break in."

"There's a restroom window around back with a broken lock," Frank said. "I can climb in and open the door for you."

"Good idea," the lieutenant agreed. "That'll save smashing in a door. But just in case anyone is inside, I'd rather send a policeman instead of you."

He designated one of the officers to go to the back and enter through the restroom window. A few minutes later, the officer unlocked the front door.

"Nobody in the place, sir," he reported.

Lieutenant Frisby led the way into the warehouse. When he saw the three cars and the row of engines, he stopped short and stared. "Well, I'll be," he muttered, then turned to the boys. "My apologies, gentlemen."

"We don't blame you, Lieutenant," Frank said. "The gang was so clever, at one point they almost had *us* believing we imagined the whole thing."

The officer looked at his wristwatch. "After five-thirty. It's unlikely any of the gang will return here tonight, and Admax will be closed by now. I'll have both places watched. We'll nab the crooks as soon as they show up in the morning."

"We know a couple of stakeout points, one in front and one in back," Joe said.

"Good."

The boys showed the officer the cardboard refrigerator carton near the front door and the shed across the alley. The lieutenant posted a man with a walkie-talkie in each place and told them he would have a backup force of several squad cars waiting nearby. They were to move in as soon as the stakeouts reported that the gang had arrived the next morning.

Frank spoke up. "There are a couple of other places you ought to watch, too, Lieutenant. We know where Red Sluice lives, and have the address of his girlfriend's apartment. I think Anton Jivaro is staying with Red."

"The hijacker?" the lieutenant said. "We want him as badly as the gang members."

"He *is* a gang member," Vern said as Frank gave the officer the two addresses, which he wrote in a notebook.

"Maybe you ought to keep all four places under surveillance and hold off making arrests for a few days," Fenton Hardy suggested. "If you move in right away, you may miss the kingpin of the operation. But if you maintain a stakeout, he might show up. If he doesn't, one of the gang members might lead you to him."

"In the meantime, they'll tear apart my car," Vern said ruefully.

"You can identify the big boss from the picture I took," Frank said. "I'll have it developed tomorrow and turn it over to you."

The lieutenant looked doubtful. "I'd rather not wait to move in at any of the locations, but we won't tip our hands. We'll stay out of sight and nab them as they show up. That way none of them will have the opportunity to spread the alarm. Of course, they'll know something's up when people start disappearing. Still, it should only take a few days to net all of them."

Mr. Hardy smiled. "I guess my investigation of the theft ring is over. Lieutenant, I'll give you the information I have, including the descriptions of all known gang members. That should wrap it up. From there on it will merely be a matter of nabbing them."

"I certainly appreciate your help, Mr. Hardy," the lieutenant said.

"You're welcome. Boys, are you ready to fly back to Bayport with me tonight?"

"I don't think so," Joe said. "We still have the mystery of Vern's coin to solve. Up till now, we haven't had much time to concentrate on that."

"Besides," Vern added, "I want to hang around to

wait for my car. When can I have it back, Lieutenant?" he asked eagerly.

"Tomorrow," the lieutenant replied. "It will be in the police impound lot."

"Well, boys," Mr. Hardy said, "perhaps you can take me to the hotel to pick up my baggage, and then drive me to the airport."

He shook hands with the lieutenant and said good-bye. The officer told the boys to phone him the next day. "I'll let you know how successful the stakeout was," he promised.

In the morning, Frank took his film to a twenty-four-hour developing service. Then, he phoned Lieutenant Frisby from their hotel room, holding the receiver so that the other boys could hear the conversation.

"So far we've had only partial success," the lieutenant reported. "A number of small frys were arrested at the warehouse, but they were just workers employed to strip the stolen cars. At Admax, we nabbed the man who claimed to be Osgood Admax, and who turned out to be a wanted forger named Calvin Renk. His clerk, Melvin, apparently was just an employee, and didn't know the items they sold were stolen."

"You haven't gotten Big Harry, Crafty Kraft, Red Sluice, or Anton Jivaro yet?" Frank asked.

"No, nor the big boss. Neither Sluice nor Jivaro has been near Red's house, Red hasn't visited his girlfriend, and none of them have shown up at either the warehouse or the store."

"You think they were somehow tipped off?"

"No, I suspect they are simply being cautious. They are a cagier group than I thought. Probably they just went underground for a few days to make sure they really had me fooled. I'm suddenly not too confident that we'll get them anytime soon."

"Why, Lieutenant?"

"Before they surface, they'll take the precaution of phoning the store to speak to Calvin Renk, and the warehouse to ask for one of the workmen there. When they can't get hold of either, I think they'll run!"

18 A Surprising Discovery

Vern said to Frank, "Let me speak to the lieutenant before you hang up."

"Hold on, Lieutenant," Frank said. "Vern Nelson wants to talk to you."

He handed the phone to his friend.

"When can I get my car back, sir?" Vern asked.

Come down and sign for it anytime you want. Check in here first and I'll have the papers ready for you. But not before 2:00 P.M., because I'm leaving for lunch."

"All right," Vern said. "We'll see you at two."

The boys ate at the hotel coffee shop, then drove to Parker Center. They found Lieutenant Frisby in the auto-theft division squad room. When Vern had signed the necessary papers, the lieutenant gave him a release form to present at the impound lot in return for his car.

"One other thing, Lieutenant," Vern said. "Do you think we could get a look at a certain case file?"

"Which one?"

"A missing 1913 Liberty Head nickel that disappeared. It was left to me by my uncle, Gregg Nelson, but wasn't in his safe-deposit box when it was opened."

"That would be a case for the burglary division," the lieutenant said, picking up his phone.

After a short conversation, he hung up. "No such complaint was ever filed," he announced.

The boys looked at each other. Joe said, "Maybe we'd better ask the lawyer who handled your uncle's estate about that, Vern."

The boys thanked Lieutenant Frisby, then got Vern's car released from the impound lot. Since they did not need two cars, they turned in the rented one.

"What's our next move?" Chet asked as they drove away from the rental agency.

"There's nothing more we can do about the gang," Frank said, "so we're free to concentrate on Vern's nickel. Who is this lawyer Joe mentioned?"

"Charles Avery in the Nichols Building," Vern

said. "It sure sounds fishy that he never reported the coin missing."

They found Charles Avery in his seventeenth-floor office. Vern introduced Frank and Chet, and the plump attorney invited them all to sit down.

Vern said, "We just came from the police, Mr. Avery. How come you never reported that the coin was missing?"

"Because there was no evidence that a crime had been committed," the lawyer said smoothly. "For all we know, your uncle hid the nickel somewhere other than in the safe-deposit box."

"But his will said he put it there."

Mr. Avery nodded. "On the other hand, there was no evidence of the box having been tampered with. Did you talk to Bank President Laing?"

"Yes."

"And he was no help?"

Vern said ruefully, "He explained to us how impossible it was for anyone but Uncle Gregg to get in that safe-deposit box."

"Actually that only increases the mystery, doesn't it? I don't see how the police could have done anything, even if I had reported it."

"They could have checked coin dealers to see if the nickel was offered for sale," Joe suggested.

Pursing his lips, the lawyer said, "I hadn't thought of that."

146

"We could check them now," Frank suggested. "Let's make a list of all coin dealers in the area, and visit every one of them."

"You can use my telephone directory," Charles Avery offered.

The boys looked in the yellow pages and copied down a list of names.

"This is going to take a long time," Chet said, as they finished.

"Perhaps you ought to start with the dealer through whom Mr. Nelson bought the coin," the lawyer suggested. "I have it in my file." He rose to get a folder from a cabinet and leafed through it. "Here it is," he commented. "Everett Fox on Wilshire Boulevard."

"I thought he bought it from a fellow collector in Massachusetts," Vern spoke up.

Mr. Avery nodded. "But it was handled through a local dealer on a commission basis. Such sales usually are."

He wrote the address of Fox's shop on a scrap of paper and handed it to Vern.

As they left the building, Chet said darkly, "That explanation of why he didn't make a police report sounds fishy to me. I think he's the one who swiped the coin."

"We'll need more evidence before we make any accusations," Frank said.

147

They drove to the address on Wilshire Boulevard. There was a barred plate-glass window with FOX COIN AND STAMP COMPANY lettered on it. Inside, two long counters ran from front to rear on either side of the store. A fussy-looking little man with gold-rimmed eyeglasses stood behind one of them, waiting on a fat woman.

"Be with you gentlemen in a minute," he said as the boys came in.

"No hurry," Frank told him.

The two counters were glass-topped. The one on the right contained displays of postage stamps. The left one was devoted to coins.

Chet studied the display. It consisted mostly of single coins, but in some cases there were complete collections in flat, plastic-covered folders.

"You know," Chet said, "this is a hobby that could be a lot of fun."

Joe whispered to Vern, "Here we go again. Chet's going to develop a new interest."

"Does he do that often?"

"About once a month. He gets all enthusiastic about something, then drops it."

Looking over his shoulder, Chet asked, "Are you guys talking about me?"

"I was just betting your cousin that you're about to become a coin expert," Joe replied.

"Not in a big way. I thought maybe I'd just collect

some ordinary coins, like this penny collection here."

He pointed to a pair of three-section folders lying open. When the other boys crowded around to look, they saw that they were Lincoln Head pennies.

"There can't be more than a hundred and fifty pennies there," Chet said. "I can afford a dollar and a half."

Vern said, "You don't get a collection like that at face value, Chet. Count on it costing a lot more."

"I suppose coin dealers have to make their profit," Chet conceded. "I don't mind paying a fair premium."

The woman customer left and the fussy little man came over to them.

"I'm Everett Fox," he said. "How may I help you gentlemen?"

Pointing to the penny collection, Chet said, "I'm interested in that."

"A fine collection," the coin dealer said, rubbing his hands together. "That's the Lincoln penny with wheat ears on the reverse, minted from 1909 to 1959. One hundred and forty-three coins altogether."

Frank said, "It was only fifty years from 1909 to 1959. How come so many coins?"

"There are different mint marks, because they

were struck at different mints. For instance in just the first year there were four: the 1909 V.D.B.; the 1909 S, V.D.B.; the plain 1909; and the 1909 S."

"What do all those letters mean?" Chet asked.

"V.D.B. are the initials of the designer, which appeared on only two issues. S is the San Francisco mint, and when there is no mint mark, it means the coin was minted in Philadelphia."

"I see," Chet said. "How much for the whole collection?"

"These are all either proof coins or uncirculated," the dealer said. "Sold individually they would cost you about eight. As a complete collection, naturally their value increases. I'm asking eleven."

"Eleven dollars?" Chet said dubiously. "For only a dollar-forty-three cents worth of pennies? I don't know."

"Not eleven dollars," the coin dealer said, elevating his nose. "Eleven thousand."

Chet gulped.

Frank chuckled. "I can loan you ten bucks, Chet. You could put the rest on your credit card."

Joe said to Vern, "That's a record. He had this hobby for less than five minutes."

Frank addressed Mr. Fox. "Actually, we came in to talk about a 1913 Liberty Head nickel."

"Oh, are you making a bid?" the dealer asked.

"A bid on what?"

"The nickel currently being offered for auction by the DuBois estate in Paris."

"We hadn't heard about that," Frank said. "When did DuBois acquire the coin?"

"Oh, it's been in his collection for over fifty years."

The boys looked at each other. "I guess that rules out it being Uncle Gregg's," Vern said.

The coin dealer said, "If you want to make a bid, I will be glad to forward it."

"How much would we have to bid?" Frank asked.

"The last auction for such a coin was eight years ago, and a man named Gregg Nelson got it for a hundred thousand dollars. He outbid the next-highest bidder by only two thousand."

"Who was that?" Joe asked.

"A local banker and avid coin collector named Barton Laing!"

19 The Big Boss

"Barton Laing!" Vern exclaimed.

"You know the man?" Everett Fox asked.

Vern nodded grimly.

"Strange thing," the coin dealer said. "Naturally, I contacted him when this auction was announced, and he expressed no interest at all."

"Maybe because he already has a Liberty Head nickel," Joe muttered under his breath.

"Beg pardon?" Mr. Fox asked.

"Just talking to myself," Joe replied.

Frank spoke up. "What would you do if someone walked in and offered you a 1913 Liberty Head nickel?"

"Have him arrested," Mr. Fox said promptly. "There are only five known to exist, and I know who the owners of all of those are. It would have to be stolen."

"Any other dealer would have the same reaction?" Frank persisted.

"Any honest one." After a pause Mr. Fox said reflectively, "I doubt that even a dishonest dealer would take a chance. The moment he offered it for sale, *he* would be arrested."

"Then actually there wouldn't be much point in stealing such a coin, would there?"

"Not for profit. An unscrupulous collector might steal one for his own collection."

"Thank you for the information," Frank said. "Let's go, fellows."

Outside, Joe said, "Seems pretty obvious who stole Vern's coin. I don't think we have to waste time visiting any other dealers."

"But how are we going to prove it?" Chet asked.

"I have an idea," Frank said. "I noticed a little park only about a block from here. Let's go sit on a bench and talk about it."

"That's Pershing Square you're talking about," Vern said. "Down that way." He pointed left.

They walked to Pershing Square and found a vacant bench.

"Okay, guru," Chet said to Frank. "We await your words of wisdom."

Frank smiled. "Barton Laing has never met me or

Chet. Suppose Chet phoned him and pretended to be a fellow bank president? He could say he has a son interested in coins, and ask if Mr. Laing would be kind enough to show the young man his collection."

"And you're the son?" Joe asked.

"Right."

"Two objections. Barton Laing probably knows most of the other bank presidents in town. If we used a real name, it might be a personal friend of his. If we gave a fake name, he might catch on, knowing the bank and the name of the president."

"That's only one objection," Frank said.

"I know. The other is that Chet's voice sounds too young to belong to a bank president."

"No problem," Frank said. "He can pretend to be calling long distance from somewhere like San Diego, and he can make his voice low."

"Laing still might know the names of all the banks in the state," Joe said. "And probably he has a directory that lists their presidents. He'd be almost sure to look it up after the call."

"So let's pick an actual San Diego bank and use the real name of its president," Vern suggested. "We'll take the chance that Laing doesn't know him personally."

They all looked at him. "How do we do that?" Chet inquired.

"It's simple," Vern said. "Just follow me."

He led the way up Fifth Street to the Los Angeles Public Library only a block away. There he went to a shelf of telephone directories.

"They have one for every major city in the country," he said. "I found out the library had them when I was visiting my uncle once and wanted the address of a friend in Vermont. He sent me down here."

Vern took the San Diego directory and carried it to a table. From the yellow pages they picked out a bank called the Bouchercon Trust Company, and Vern wrote down the number.

"Anybody got a couple of dollars worth of change?" he inquired.

The boys searched their pockets and came up with three dollars in nickels, dimes, and quarters.

"That should be enough," Vern said. "It's only a little over a hundred miles."

There were several public phones in the library, and he called the San Diego bank.

"Will you tell me the name of your president, please?" he asked when a woman answered.

"Certainly, sir. It's Mr. Jason McGuire. Do you wish to speak to him?"

"Not right now, thanks," Vern said, and hung up.

"A piece of cake." He grinned. "The president's name is Jason McGuire."

"You may as well phone from here, Chet," Frank suggested. "Let's hear your executive voice."

In a low, false bass Chet said, "This is Jason McGuire, Mr. Laing."

A passing librarian gave him a sharp look, and Joe chuckled. "You sound more like a bank robber disguising his voice. We better go outside to practice."

Several people were seated on the library lawn, reading. The boys moved out of earshot of everyone, and Chet practiced several different voices. They all sounded false, but suddenly Joe had an idea.

"Why don't you develop laryngitis?" he suggested. "That way, if Laing happens to know Mr. McGuire, you'll have an excuse for your voice being different."

In a hoarse, rasping tone Chet said, "Sorry if I'm hard to understand, old chap, but I've got laryngitis."

"That's perfect," Frank said approvingly.

They went back in and Chet phoned the Bunker Bank, asking for Barton Laing.

"Who's calling, please?" the switchboard operator asked.

"Jason McGuire, of Bouchercon Trust in San Diego."

"Just a moment, please."

156

Then a hearty voice sounded in Chet's ear. "How are you, Jason, old man?"

Barton Laing was obviously acquainted with the San Diego bank president and for a moment threw Chet off balance. The boy almost answered in his normal tone, but just in time he remembered and said hoarsely, "Fine, except for laryngitis."

"You sound terrible," Laing said with sympathy.

"I'll keep it brief, Bart, because it's hard for me to talk. Do you know my son Frank?"

"Not unless he was at some bankers' convention with you. I've never been in your home."

Chet was relieved. "Frank has the same hobby you do, coin collecting. He's driving up there from San Diego this afternoon, and I wonder if you'd do me the favor of letting him see your collection."

"I'll be glad to," Barton Laing said, apparently pleased. "We coin nuts like nothing better than to show off our treasures. When will he be here?"

"He's leaving now, so it shouldn't be more than a couple of hours. It's not quite three. He should make it by five."

"Maybe he'd like to drop over for dinner about seven, Jason? We'd love to have him."

Chet panicked and almost choked. "Ah, no, ah, he has a dinner date with friends. Could he come later?"

"Sure," Barton Laing said. "Tell him to make it

eight, then." He gave an address in West Los Angeles.

"Thanks very much," Chet said. "He'll be there."

"Take care of that laryngitis," Laing said, "and good-bye."

When Chet hung up, Joe slapped him on the back. "You did a wonderful job!"

"Thanks," Chet rasped. Then he looked surprised. "I-I think my voice stuck!"

"A soda should fix you up," Frank told him.

Chet cleared his throat and said in his normal tone, "I've recovered, but I'll still take that soda."

They found a small restaurant on Fifth Street, across from Pershing Square, and sat in a booth. Over cold drinks they discussed the coin case.

"Even as bank president," Vern said, "I don't see how Laing could have gotten into that box, because Uncle Gregg's key was needed."

"He didn't necessarily have to steal it himself," Joe pointed out. "Maybe he just bought it from the thief."

"You mean Cylvia Nash?"

"It makes more sense than Laing personally taking it," Joe said. "Suppose Cylvia, knowing that her boss would do nearly anything to get the coin for his collection, slipped it out of your uncle's box after he handed it back to her to lock it up. She could have taken it while she was walking away from him with the box and her back was turned to him. He wouldn't know it was missing because he never checked the box after that."

"I think you've got it," Frank said. "That fifty-thousand-dollar deposit in Cylvia Nash's savings account must be what Laing paid her for the coin. It all fits."

"All except her being the girlfriend of Red Sluice," Chet said. "How does *he* figure in this?"

"He doesn't have to fit into the coin theft," Joe told him. "Birds of a feather flock together. Probably they met each other because they travel in the same circles."

The house in West Los Angeles was an expensive home on an exclusive street. Vern parked a quarter block away and Frank got out alone.

"I shouldn't be long," he said. "As soon as I spot your coin, Vern, I'll make an excuse to leave and we'll drive straight to Parker Center."

He mounted the steps to the wide veranda and rang the bell.

The door was opened by a distinguished-looking man, and Frank gaped. It was the same man he had photographed entering the warehouse!

20 The Missing Coin

Trying to control his expression, Frank asked, "Mr. Laing?"

"Yes," the banker said cordially, holding out his hand. "You must be Frank McGuire."

"Yes, sir," Frank said, shaking hands. Barton Laing led him through a front room into a library and offered him a seat. Frank took a leather-covered easy chair, while the banker sat behind a desk.

Tapping his fingers on the wood surface, the man said, "So you are a collector, too."

"Not on the same scale as you," Frank said modestly. Then, using some of the knowledge he had picked up that afternoon, he made himself sound like an expert. "My only complete set is

Lincoln Head pennies with the wheat ears on the reverse. I have all one hundred and forty-three in uncirculated coins."

"That's quite a start for a young man your age," the banker said, impressed.

"May I see your collection?" Frank urged.

Rising from his chair, Barton Laing went over to an oil painting on the wall, slid it aside to disclose a safe, and opened the box with a key. He removed a stack of blue coin folders, but left one in the safe.

Laing set the folders on the desk and carefully relocked the safe. Since nothing was left in it but a single folder, the boy couldn't help wondering why he was being so cautious.

Standing alongside of Frank, the banker now opened the folders. In descending order he displayed collections of silver dollars, half dollars, quarters, and dimes, then set them aside.

"Now come my favorites," he said, opening the first of the remaining covers. "I specialize in nickels. I have everything from the first nickel coined in the United States in 1866, the shield type, through the latest Jefferson nickel. With one or two exceptions, the sets are complete."

Looking at a folder containing Liberty Head nickels, Frank said, "This is complete except for 1913."

Barton Laing smiled. "That's not hard to under-stand, is it?"

"Not considering that there are only five in existence," Frank agreed. "Did you know that the DuBois estate is offering one for auction?"

"Yes, I heard that," Laing said. "But bidding for that is a little out of my class."

Since Frank knew the man had bid ninety-eight thousand dollars for a Liberty Head eight years ago, he figured the real reason Laing was not going to bid was that he already had the coin.

"I noticed you left one folder in the safe," Frank pointed out. "Is that something special?"

"Just an empty cover."

The doorbell rang and Barton Laing went to answer it. Frank got up to try the safe door, but it was locked tight. Quickly, he resumed his seat when he heard the banker returning.

As he entered the room, Laing said, "I have some unexpected company. Have you finished looking at everything?"

"Yes, thanks," Frank said, rising to his feet.

The banker replaced the coins in the safe and locked it. Then he gestured for Frank to precede him to the front door.

As they started through the living room, four of the five people seated there gaped at Frank.

Angrily, Big Harry Knotts, Crafty Kraft, Red Sluice, and Anton Jivaro jumped to their feet! Cylvia Nash was the only one who remained seated as the men rushed at Frank, grabbing him before a single word was said.

"What's the matter with you?" Laing asked indignantly. "How dare you manhandle my guest!"

"Do you know who he is?" Big Harry challenged.

"Certainly. Frank McGuire, the son of a colleague."

"You've got the first name right, but the last name's Hardy!"

"What!" The banker glared at Frank in outrage. "Frank Hardy! You came here to spy on me!"

Frank saw no point in replying.

"Wait here," Laing ordered his gang. "I'll be back in a minute."

He disappeared into the kitchen and returned carrying a coil of rope. "Follow me!" he said as he went past.

He led the way into the library while Frank's captors forced the boy along. Cylvia trailed after the group, her face tense.

Laing pointed to a straight-backed chair. "Tie him to that!" he ordered.

When the boy had been bound hand and foot, the banker said, "His brother and his two friends are probably nearby, too. Search the neighborhood and

163

don't let them get away. Cylvia and I'll keep our eyes on this one."

The four rushed out. Frank could hear the front door open and close. Meanwhile, Laing and Cylvia were standing side by side, watching him closely. Frank started to feel panic. How could he possibly get out of this situation? Just then, he saw a window behind his captors being pushed up slowly.

To divert their attention, he said to Cylvia, "How did a nice lady like you get involved with this gang of crooks?"

"None of your business!" Laing snapped.

"I don't get it," Frank went on. "I just don't. When we met on the airplane—"

He kept talking on and on in a loud voice, while the window was being raised all the way. Joe noiselessly threw a leg over the sill, pulled himself inside, and tiptoed up to Barton Laing. Vern was right on his heels and Chet followed.

Frank was still talking when Joe and Vern suddenly grabbed the bank president from behind. Chet ran to the doorway to block Cylvia Nash's escape in case she tried to run.

Laing struggled to get out of the boys' grip, but in vain. Vern had pushed a handkerchief into the man's mouth so he could not scream and alert his companions.

Cylvia was too scared to make a sound. She stood motionless, watching the boys subdue her boss.

"Okay, Miss Nash," Chet said. "Untie him." He pointed to Frank.

The woman gave the banker a frightened look, and went up to Frank. When he was freed, Joe and Vern forced Barton Laing down into the chair and bound and gagged him.

Then Joe turned to Cylvia. "You behave, and we won't have to do the same to you."

"I'm not going to make any trouble," she said meekly and sank into a leather love seat.

Suddenly, they heard the front door open and close, and several sets of footsteps moved their way. Chet and Frank hid on one side of the door, Joe and Vern on the other. Big Harry and his gang filed into the room. When they saw their subdued leader, they whirled to face the boys.

Frank ducked a blow from Big Harry, cracked him on the jaw, and sent him reeling backward to crash into the wall. Joe grabbed Crafty's wrist when the tattooed man swung at him, and flipped him over his shoulder onto his back, while Vern traded punches with Red Sluice.

Chet tossed little Anton Jivaro face down on the floor and sat on him. Then Big Harry bore into Frank again, swinging both fists. Frank blocked the blows, feinted, and landed another hard crack on Knotts's jaw. This time, Big Harry went down and stayed there.

Crafty started to get up, but collapsed on his face when Joe hit him with a judo chop on the side of his neck. Sluice knocked Vern off his feet and tried to kick him in the stomach. Grabbing his ankle, Vern up-ended him onto the seat of his pants. Then the Hardys grabbed the redhead and held him tight.

It wasn't until the boys had all four hoods bound securely that anyone noticed Cylvia Nash was gone!

"We should have tied her up," Chet muttered.

"Don't worry about it," Frank said. "The police will find her." He used the phone in the library to call Lieutenant Frisby. When he hung up, Vern asked, "Did you see my coin?"

"He didn't show it to me, but I think I know where it is," Frank replied. He got the safe key from the banker's pocket, unlocked the box, and lifted out all the folders except the last one. After putting them aside on the desk, he took out the remaining cover and opened it.

It contained only a single coin, a 1913 Liberty Head nickel!

"My uncle's coin!" Vern cried out.

"Well, I guess that solves both mysteries," Frank declared.

"But we haven't found the big boss of the car-theft ring yet," Joe pointed out.

"Oh, I didn't tell you? It's Laing. I was quite shocked when I came here and realized he was the man whose photo I took."

Just then, the police arrived and took the prisoners away. "We'll be on the lookout for Cylvia Nash," Lieutenant Frisby promised the boys. "Meanwhile, congratulations. You've done a great job. Sorry I didn't believe you at first. You turned out to be better detectives than we have in the department. Want to join the force?"

The boys laughed and Frank shook his head. "We'd like to know whether you get hold of Cylvia, though."

"Call me tomorrow," Frisby replied.

Cylvia Nash was arrested when she returned to her apartment that night, and the boys left town after breakfast the next morning.

"I hope you don't run into another mystery right away," Chet told the Hardys as they drove along in Vern's car. "Can't we just have some simple, plain fun for once?"

Frank and Joe grinned. "Maybe," Joe said. None of the boys knew that almost as soon as they returned to Bayport, they would find themselves involved in *The Outlaw's Silver*.

NANCY DREW® MYSTERY STORIES By Carolyn Keene

- ☐ THE TRIPLE HOAX—#57
  69153-8 $3.50
- ☐ THE FLYING SAUCER MYSTERY—#58
  72320-0 $3.50
- ☐ THE SECRET IN THE OLD LACE—#59
  69067-1 $3.99
- ☐ THE GREEK SYMBOL MYSTERY—#60
  67457-9 $3.50
- ☐ THE SWAMI'S RING—#61
  62467-9 $3.50
- ☐ THE KACHINA DOLL MYSTERY—#62
  67220-7 $3.50
- ☐ THE TWIN DILEMMA—#63
  67301-7 $3.99
- ☐ CAPTIVE WITNESS—#64
  70471-0 $3.50
- ☐ MYSTERY OF THE WINGED LION—#65
  62681-7 $3.50
- ☐ RACE AGAINST TIME—#66
  69485-5 $3.50
- ☐ THE SINISTER OMEN—#67
  73938-7 $3.50
- ☐ THE ELUSIVE HEIRESS—#68
  62478-4 $3.99
- ☐ CLUE IN THE ANCIENT DISGUISE—#69
  64279-0 $3.50
- ☐ THE BROKEN ANCHOR—#70
  74228-0 $3.50
- ☐ THE SILVER COBWEB—#71
  70992-5 $3.50
- ☐ THE HAUNTED CAROUSEL—#72
  66227-9 $3.50
- ☐ ENEMY MATCH—#73
  64283-9 $3.50
- ☐ MYSTERIOUS IMAGE—#74
  69401-4 $3.50
- ☐ THE EMERALD-EYED CAT MYSTERY—#75
  64282-0 $3.50
- ☐ THE ESKIMO'S SECRET—#76
  73003-7 $3.50
- ☐ THE BLUEBEARD ROOM—#77
  66857-9 $3.50
- ☐ THE PHANTOM OF VENICE—#78
  73422-9 $3.50
- ☐ THE DOUBLE HORROR
  OF FENLEY PLACE—#79
  64387-8 $3.50
- ☐ THE CASE OF THE DISAPPEARING
  DIAMONDS—#80
  64896-9 $3.50
- ☐ MARDI GRAS MYSTERY—#81
  64961-2 $3.50

- ☐ THE CLUE IN THE CAMERA—#82
  64962-0 $3.50
- ☐ THE CASE OF THE VANISHING VEIL—#83
  63413-5 $3.50
- ☐ THE JOKER'S REVENGE—#84
  63414-3 $3.50
- ☐ THE SECRET OF SHADY GLEN—#85
  63416-X $3.50
- ☐ THE MYSTERY OF MISTY CANYON—#86
  63417-8 $3.99
- ☐ THE CASE OF THE RISING STARS—#87
  66312-7 $3.50
- ☐ THE SEARCH FOR CINDY AUSTIN—#88
  66313-5 $3.50
- ☐ THE CASE OF THE DISAPPEARING DEEJAY—#89
  66314-3 $3.50
- ☐ THE PUZZLE AT PINEVIEW SCHOOL—#90
  66315-1 $3.95
- ☐ THE GIRL WHO COULDN'T REMEMBER—#91
  66316-X $3.50
- ☐ THE GHOST OF CRAVEN COVE—#92
  66317-8 $3.50
- ☐ THE CASE OF THE SAFECRACKER'S SECRET—#93
  66318-6 $3.50
- ☐ THE PICTURE PERFECT MYSTERY—#94
  66315-1 $3.50
- ☐ THE SILENT SUSPECT—#95
  69280-1 $3.50
- ☐ THE CASE OF THE PHOTO FINISH—#96
  69281-X $3.99
- ☐ THE MYSTERY AT MAGNOLIA MANSION—#97
  69282-8 $3.99
- ☐ THE HAUNTING OF HORSE ISLAND—#98
  69284-4 $3.50
- ☐ THE SECRET AT SEVEN ROCKS—#99
  69285-2 $3.50
- ☐ A SECRET IN TIME—#100
  69286-0 $3.50
- ☐ THE MYSTERY OF THE MISSING MILLIONAIRESS—#101
  69287-9 $3.50
- ☐ THE SECRET IN THE DARK—#102
  69279-8 $3.50
- ☐ THE STRANGER IN THE SHADOWS—#103
  73049-5 $3.50
- ☐ THE MYSTERY OF THE JADE TIGER—#104
  73050-9 $3.50
- ☐ THE CLUE IN THE ANTIQUE TRUNK—#105
  73051-7 $3.99
- ☐ THE CASE OF THE ARTFUL CRIME—#106
  73052-5 $3.99
- ☐ NANCY DREW® GHOST STORIES—#1
  69132-5 $3.50

and don't forget...THE HARDY BOYS® Now available in paperback

Simon & Schuster, Mail Order Dept. ND5
200 Old Tappan Road, Old Tappan, NJ 07675
Please send me copies of the books checked. Please add appropriate local sales tax.
☐ Enclosed full amount per copy with this coupon (Send
check or money order only.)

☐ If order is for $10.00 or more, you
may charge to one of the following
accounts:

Please be sure to include proper postage and handling:

☐ Mastercard   ☐ Visa

95¢—first copy
50¢—each additonal copy ordered.

Name _____ Credit Card No. _____

Address _____

City _____ Card Expiration Date _____

State _____ Zip _____ Signature _____
Books listed are also available at your local bookstore. Prices are subject to change without notice.   NDD-45